PAINT ME

AN EROTIC ADVENTURE

VICTORIA RUSH

VOLUME 14

JADE'S EROTIC ADVENTURES - BOOK 14

COPYRIGHT

Paint Me © 2019 Victoria Rush

Cover Design © 2019 PhotoMaras

FEEL THE RUSH:

Jade's Erotic Adventures – Book 1

When lonely divorcée Jade seeks to broaden her horizons, she's invited to a private dinner event which promises to stimulate all of her senses. Wearing nothing but masquerade masks, dinner guests receive special service under the table while their fellow diners look on...

The Dinner Party

Jade's Erotic Adventures - Book 2

Jade discovers an exotic adventure club where strangers meet to explore each other's bodies in mysterious dark rooms. Using special effects to project swirling light patterns onto their figures, the shifting shadows provide just enough illumination to highlight their naked bodies while protecting their identities...

The Dark Room

Jade's Erotic Adventures - Book 3

Jade discovers a yoga club where members stretch and explore each other's bodies in the buff. She books an appointment, and during the first session meets a young redhead who tantalizes her with her flexibility and stunning body...

Naked Yoga

For the uninhibited...

1

CREATIVE LICENSE

I t had been weeks since I'd felt the live touch of another woman and I was beginning to feel restless. There was only so long I could go relying on my own devices for fulfillment, even with the help of live online partners. I needed to experience the excitement of a warm body next to me, one who responded to my touch just as I was to hers. I wanted to feel her hot breath on my skin, her moisture on my lips, and her moans in my ear.

One recent day after clearing through the checkout line at the grocery store, an intriguing poster caught my attention on the bulletin board near the exit. It had a photo of a buxom beauty dressed in a Wonder Woman costume with the headline *Looking for a New Adventure?* I stopped my cart and leaned in to admire the girl's curvy figure. Her uniform was so intricately detailed and form-fitting, it almost looked like it was painted on her. The stylized 'W' emblem on her chest arched over her firm breasts and her star-spangled briefs hugged every curve of her hourglass-shaped hips.

I'd never seen a woman in costume look so sexy and striking. As I squinted at the picture ogling her centerfold-perfect figure, I gasped when I recognized the telltale dimples and bulges on her body. At the edge of the black outline surrounding her chest emblem there were two raised nubs located in the center of each breast, and in the middle of her gold belt buckle was a little indentation right where her belly button should be. Even in the crotch of her tight blue shorts, I could make out the tiny appendage of her clitoris poking seductively between her splayed legs. I grasped the handle of my grocery cart, suddenly becoming weak at the knees.

That's not a uniform she's wearing, I thought. *She's naked! That costume is actually painted on her body!*

As I began reading the banner description to see what it was all about, my panties flooded with moisture:

Embrace your inner superhero—join our nude body painting workshop and experience the thrill of living out your wildest fantasies in the flesh. Explore your artistic side using the beautiful human form as your canvas. You can choose to be either the painter-voyeur or the model-exhibitionist. Bring a friend or partner up with one of our like-minded muses at our private studio. Either way, you'll find this to be an unparalleled experience. Find more details at nudebodypainting.com.

By the time I finished reading the ad, the front of my jeans was soaked with a giant wet spot. I found the idea of painting a beautiful naked body up close and having someone do the same to me incredibly arousing. If their customers looked anything like the Wonder Woman model, I couldn't wait to lay my brush—or my hands—on her naked body. This forum was a perfect fit with my graphic design skills. Except this time, I'd be exploring my passion for illustration with live brush and oil.

Holding my cart close to my hips to conceal the stain between my legs, I wheeled the buggy to my car and quickly drove home to gather more information about this intriguing class. When I opened the website, I was greeted with a gallery of colorful men and women bodypainted in a variety of themes. Some were covered in nature motifs with beautiful flowers and foliage covering every square inch of their bodies. Others appeared to be wearing professional uniforms that looked as authentic as the real thing. And there were plenty more superhero costumes, ranging from Batman and Superman to Catwoman and Elastagirl.

In every instance, the designs were so detailed and intricate that it was difficult to separate their naked private parts from the rest of their figures. Extra embellishment was added to their erogenous zones in a concerted effort to disguise their nudity. But as I zoomed in on each picture, it was impossible not to notice the little shadows betrayed by their bare nipples and navels. Most of the men appeared to be wearing a codpiece, but at least one brave model painted as *The Thing* let it all hang out with the creative placement of orange-colored stones coating his genitals.

As I scrolled further down the page viewing more pictures showing artists applying their brushes to the naked figures of their models, my panties clung to my rapidly moistening vulva. I imagined caressing my model's nipples with the soft brush hairs, watching them harden and elongate as I swirled the dye around her areolas. What a turn-on it must be to feel the wet oil being dabbled on the most private areas of your body! I slid my hand down my panties and rubbed my fingers along my slick lips, trying to imagine the sensation.

But I still had many questions about how the program worked. *What happens if the model gets excited while they're being painted? How could anyone not feel aroused with someone caressing your private parts with a soft, moist brush?* I imagined the studio filled with soft moans and sighs as the male models' penises hardened and the female models' hips gyrated from the pleasurable sensations.

And what becomes of the models when the artist's composition is finally finished? I thought. It would be a shame to have to wash it all off before leaving the studio. I'd want to take my newly fashioned superhero into a private room and have my way with her as I fantasized about her using her superpowers on me. Suddenly, a Live Chat box opened in the lower corner of the website window, and an ellipsis appeared, indicated someone was sending me a message.

Hi, I'm Eva, the attendant typed. *Can I answer any questions you might have about our program?*

I removed my wet hand from between my legs and wiped it on the front of my jeans, then placed my fingers over the keyboard.

Yes, I began. *What happens if I come to the studio alone? How do I pair up with a partner?*

My clit throbbed in anticipation as I watched Eva typing her reply.

We try to schedule even numbers of participants for each session to ensure everybody has a partner. But in the event there's a last-minute cancelation or no-show, the workshop instructor will stand in for anyone who's orphaned.

Stand in? I thought. If the instructor looks anything like the gorgeous Wonder Woman model on their poster, I'd volunteer to be one of the orphans any day.

How long is each session? I asked. *Do both partners get painted by the time it ends?*

We schedule two hours for each session, Eva replied. *Most clients need the full allotment of time to cover a complete body with a detailed design. Although some artists can work more quickly, our customers find it's more relaxing and rewarding to devote all of their attention to one partner at a time. We offer a discount for follow-up sessions to encourage you to take your time and use the full allocation to create a truly memorable experience.*

Memorable experience indeed, I thought. I could only imagine how worked up both the artist and the model would get after two full hours of worshipping their partner's bodies in such close quarters.

Are we allowed to use any design of our choosing?

Absolutely. We encourage our artists to be creative. But if you have trouble finding inspiration, you can choose from a large number of interesting templates we have in our design catalogue.

My mind had already begun racing ahead with risqué ideas for my models.

I'm an experienced graphic designer, so I probably won't need too much help with that aspect of the procedure. But what happens if my partner needs some assistance?

That's what the workshop coach is for. She's available for coaching support during the duration of the session. Even if she's busy with her own client, you can still ask her questions at any time and she can pull away to provide personal help.

I smiled, imagining how far the 'personal help' might go in such a sexually-charged atmosphere.

Are the models always fully naked?

It's generally more fun to have the full canvas to work with, but we don't pressure anyone to be entirely naked. If customers wish to cover up their private areas with tight-fitting undergarments, that is their prerogative. Oftentimes it's difficult to tell they're wearing any clothing once the design is fully blended in.

I pinched my eyebrows wondering how safe it would be to allow paint to invade our private spaces.

What kind of paint do you use? Is it non-toxic and hypoallergenic?

We have three different types of paint, depending on how long you wish for it to remain on your body. The easiest to work with is an oil-based paint that goes on smoothly and is quick to wash off. But some clients like to wear their design a little longer and carry it home under loose clothing to show their friends and lovers. For this, we have a latex-based paint that hardens to a rubbery coating that you can peel off. We also have a vegetable-based paint that enables your partner to remove the coating in a more exciting manner. In all cases, the paint is fully hypoallergenic and non-toxic.

Edible paint? Holy shit! I thought. That would really allow me to let my imagination run wild with my superhero muse. But I wondered if the studio environment would be appropriate if my partner and I wanted to go that far.

How open are the workshop participants to that kind of activity, or is that something that's meant to be reserved for the privacy of one's own home?

Most of our customers find the experience of having their naked bodies painted by someone else to be highly stimulating. Plus, it takes a certain kind of free spirit to disrobe in front of a bunch of other strangers and allow your most intimate areas to be touched in this manner. We find that most clients are quite open to the unrestricted exploration of their bodies before, during, and after the actual painting process. But if you want more privacy, we also have private cubicles and showers in the change rooms for your personal use.

I began to feel my panties sticking to my thighs and looked between my legs, seeing another wet patch forming in the crotch of my jeans. The whole idea of painting nude models in the open space of a group studio was incredibly erotic. The thought of licking my muse clean after I finished painting her with a beautiful design was just the icing on the cake. I quickly wrapped up my online chat so I could attend to more pressing matters.

I think you've convinced me this is something I'd like to try, I typed with trembling hands. *How do I go about making an appointment?*

Just choose an available date and time, then fill in the online booking form under the Appointments tab and make your payment. Feel free to book either a couples session or a solo appointment. Either way, we'll make sure you're partnered up with a like-minded partner. But keep in mind that sessions fill up quickly since we limit each class size to ten participants. Hope to see you soon!

I booked an appointment for next Saturday, then signed out of the chat session and ran downstairs, scrambling through my kitchen cupboards looking for some kind of makeshift body paint. The best I could find was a few small tubes of food dye and a small jar of blackberry jam. Then I smiled when I noticed a large tub of peanut butter in the pantry. I stripped off my clothes and rubbed the batter all over my tits and stomach, watching myself in the hallway mirror. As I swirled the paste into a faux bodice and panty design mimicking the sexy Wonder Woman figure on the bodypainting poster, I spread my legs and rolled my burning clit between my fingers. In a matter of seconds, I came hard imagining myself licking the sticky substance off my moaning partner.

2

PAINTING OUTSIDE THE LINES

When I arrived at the bodypainting studio on the day of my scheduled appointment, I was trembling in excitement. I still wasn't sure exactly what to expect, but I knew it was unlikely to be anything like any of my previous art classes. I'd done a few nude studies before, but this took the idea of illustrating a naked body to an entirely new level. This time I'd be touching my model up close and personal, using her body as my very own canvas.

As customers streamed into the salon, I sized up each person as a potential partner. Most of the participants wore full-length clothing, so it was difficult to imagine their bodies naked and exposed under the bright lights of the studio environment. But I saw enough curvy hips and shapely breasts under their tight jeans and blouses to rekindle the memory of my body plastered in peanut butter.

Unfortunately, most of the visitors appeared to be already paired up as couples. Three of the pairs were young men and women who were obviously looking for a little adventure to spice up their love life. But one of the couples was a middle-aged lesbian pair who peered at me expectantly as they entered the room. The chunky blue-haired butch eyed me up and down, but her pretty girlfriend smiled at me as her partner led her by her hand. She couldn't have been much older than me, and I felt myself blushing as I checked out her slim dancer's figure in her skinny jeans.

That left me the odd woman out watching the hostess greet each new couple as they entered the studio. She looked to be in her early 30s with long blonde hair tied back in a ponytail. Her bright green eyes and pretty smile reminded me of the actress Charlize Theron, but her figure was all Sofia Vergara. Her full breasts created a deep cleavage in her tight-fitting blouse, and her curvy hips swayed seductively as she greeted each new guest. I glanced up at the clock, remembering the online chat attendant saying each session was limited to ten participants. With only a few minutes left, I squeezed my thighs together in anticipation of being paired up with the instructor.

But just as she moved to lock the front door behind the blacked-out windows, a young girl who barely looked out of her teens squeezed through the entrance. The moment I looked at her, she took my breath away. With shimmering auburn hair, large radiant eyes and pale freckled skin, she looked like the consummate girl next door. Fresh-faced and perky with an infectious smile, I was instantly smitten by her, quickly abandoning the notion of partnering up with the instructor. Besides, I thought, she had a more suitable palette for the design concept I'd been mulling over for my model the last few days.

With all the scheduled participants now accounted for, the hostess latched the front door and moved to the front of room.

"Good morning, everyone," she said, peering around the room. "My name's Molly and I'll be your facilitator for today's class. Thank you all for coming. I think you'll find this workshop to be a unique and exhilarating experience. It looks like everybody's already paired up except for Jade and Brianna, so if you two would like to introduce yourselves, we can get started in just a few minutes."

I looked over in the direction of the pretty redhead and she glanced back at me shyly. She seemed frozen in her corner of the room so I strolled over and introduced myself.

"Hi, I'm Jade," I said, extending my hand slowly.

"I'm Bree," the girl said in a gentle voice. "Pleased to meet you."

When our hands touched, I could feel the perspiration on her palm. I wasn't sure if she was more nervous about the prospect of getting naked in front of a bunch of strangers or from being one of the only orphans along with me. As a show of solidarity, I held her hand as I turned back to face Molly.

"Before I explain some of the logistics and protocols for our workshop," she said, "does anyone have any general questions? I know this can seem a bit daunting at first, since I believe this is a first-time experience for all of you."

One of the couples asked a question about how easy it was to remove the paint from their bodies, and I absent-mindedly glanced around the workshop. There were five distinct stations positioned about ten feet apart, each with a large easel and table carrying an assortment of bowls, paint canisters and different-sized brushes. The easels had a large sketchpad overlaid by a roll of cellophane sheets depicting various characters and images from the public eye. Some of the pictures displayed familiar superhero characters, while others showed famous reproductions of classical portraits from painters ranging from Picasso to Warhol to Vermeer. I smiled, remembering the unique design that I had envisioned from one of my own favorite artists.

"Right, then," Molly said when she finished answering the last of the participant questions. "If each of you wants to stake out a position next to one of the easels scattered around the room, let me explain how to use the materials. You'll find a variety of bowls and brushes at each of your tables, together with a collection of different colored paint canisters. These aren't the typical oil paints you find in the art store. Because you'll be painting on a larger and smoother canvas, i.e. your own bodies, we use a special fluid-acrylic type that spreads and binds more easily to naked skin.

"I suggest that you pour small quantities of each color you wish to use into the empty bowls, then select the fineness of each brush depending on how detailed your design. The broad brushes allow you to cover more area with a uniform pattern, and the thin brushes allow you to apply more detailed designs. There's also a bowl filled with clear water to clean your brushes when changing from one color to another. You also have an easel to draw some preliminary sketches if you wish and a variety of design templates to peruse for inspiration. I'll be circulating around the room and offering assistance whenever you need it, but feel free to shout out any questions as they come up. We've intentionally kept our group size small so I can give you more personalized attention.

"All you need to do now is decide who's going to start off being the painter and who will be the muse. Take your time and have fun. You'll likely find you need the full two hours to finish painting your partner's full body, in which case you can swap positions at our next class. There's a clean smock on each table, which I highly encourage the painter to use to protect your clothing. Now let's get this party started!"

Bree and I stepped toward the nearest painter's station and glanced at each other uncertainly. I didn't have any hesitation about stripping naked in front of other people, but I could tell that she was feeling a bit nervous.

"What role were you thinking you'd like to play first?" I asked.

Bree raised her eyebrows and frowned.

"I'm not much of an artist," she said, peering at my gym-toned body. "I'm afraid I wouldn't be able to do your beautiful figure proper justice."

"Not to worry," I smiled, happy she was giving me an opportunity to touch her first. "I've actually got a little experience in this area, so it might be easier for me to go first." I stared at her little buds poking under her tight t-shirt, trying to contain my excitement. "That is, if you don't mind taking off your clothes..."

Bree hesitated for a moment, glancing down at the floor.

"Do you mind if keep myself partially covered?" she said. "I've got a tight sports bra and some thong panties that shouldn't get in the way too much—"

"No worries," I squinted, disappointed that she wasn't going to give me complete access to her girlish figure. "We can make it work either way."

"Okay. Where do you want me to stand?"

I surveyed our workspace and nodded toward the area in front of a small stool next to the table.

"I suppose right here would work best. The shorter the distance from the paint and the brushes, the less mess we'll make." I paused for a moment, sizing up her figure. "Did you have any particular design in mind that you wanted me to paint?"

"Not really," she said. "If you're an experienced artist, I don't want to get in the way of your creativity. Were you thinking of anything special?"

"I had something in mind that I think perfectly suits you," I nodded. "But I'd rather keep the design a secret until I'm finished. I think it'll be all the more exciting for you to see the finished product once it's on your bare body."

"Okay," Bree said, with a curious grin. "Do you need to prepare anything?"

Sensing that she wanted a little distraction while she disrobed, I glanced toward the bowls and brushes on the side table.

"Why don't I prepare the paint while you get yourself ready?

As I opened the canisters of paint and filled five bowls with the primary colors, I listened to the rustling of Bree's clothing while she stripped. Glancing around the room, I watched each of the other models removing their clothing. Most the women chose to go completely nude, including the pretty lesbian girl on the other side of the room. The solo male model stripped down to a skimpy jockstrap covering his crotch.

Always the double-standard, I thought, shaking my head in dismay. *Perhaps his partner will be able to entice him out of this last bit of protection before they're finished.* I knew that I certainly had similar designs on my muse.

I tied the white smock around my waist then turned around to see Bree standing half-naked with her arms clasped tightly by her side. She was wearing a plain-white, one-piece bra and matching thong panties. Her pale alabaster skin looked so delicate, from a distance another observer might think she wasn't wearing anything at all. Her small but perky breasts thrust firmly against the stretchy fabric, producing two sensuous points where her aroused nipples stood. I glanced down her body and noticed the small cleft in her panties where the tight fabric hugged the indentation of her vulva. I nodded approvingly, realizing her sparse undergarments would blend in nicely with my planned design.

"You're beautiful," I said. "The perfect canvas for what I had in mind."

"You don't think the seams will interfere with your composition?"

"They might distract my *mind* a little," I smiled. "But I think we can make it work."

Bree glanced at my bowls of paint and pinched her eyebrows.

"That's a lot of yellow and black. Are you going to paint me as a leopard?"

I smiled at her and shook my head.

"Nice try, young lady," I said. "You're not going to get it out of me that easily. Though you will be nicely speckled by the time I'm finished."

"More than I already am?" she frowned self-consciously. "Don't you think I've already got enough spots?"

"Don't be silly," I said, noticing the little line of freckles running along the tan lines on her chest and hips. "You can barely see them. But in any event, they'll be all covered up by the time I'm finished. The patches I have in mind are a little more—*stylized*."

"Well now I'm intrigued," she said, spreading her legs, inviting me to begin with her lower half. "Where do you want to start?

"Let's begin at the top with your pretty face. It'll be the focal point of my composition, after all."

"Okay," Bree said, shifting her weight with a worried expression. "I didn't realize—"

"Don't worry, sweetie. I'm not going to cover you up too much. I just want to highlight certain areas of your face to add a little drama to the rest of my scheme."

I dipped a fine-hair brush into the red paint bowl and dabbled a small patch onto my palette plate, then swished it in the water bowl before adding some blue to the compound. Just then, Molly circulated by our table, watching me mix my colors.

"It looks like somebody knows her primary colors," she said, noticing Bree looking nervous as I swirled the purple mixture into my brush. "Did either of you have any questions or concerns?"

I nodded at Molly, happy that she'd arrived at an opportune moment.

"Actually, there was one thing I was wondering about. How *flexible* is this acrylic paint when it dries? I'm concerned about applying it to areas of Bree's face where changes in her expression might crack or break it."

"Good question," Molly said. "While all of our paint is safe to use on the face, if you were thinking of applying it around her eyes or mouth, you might want to consider an alternative material. We have different colors of powdered eye shadow and mascara available, as well as a full range of lip gloss colors."

"That might work a little better," I nodded. "I'll take some pink lip gloss and light purple eye shadow if you have it. And maybe a bit of rose-colored blush for her cheeks."

"Coming right up," Molly said. "I'll be back in one sec."

"*Pink and purple*, hmm?" Bree said, raising an eyebrow. "Are you painting me as a flamingo? Or a peacock, maybe?"

"Ha!" I teased. "Keep guessing—you're just going to have

to wait until the end. But I can tell you that I'm not painting you as any kind of animal."

"I figure if I just keep asking these kinds of closed questions, by the time two hours have passed I'll have figured it out simply by the process of elimination."

"You can try, girl. But this is a pretty unique design. I'll be surprised if you've seen it before."

"How do you know I'll like it then?"

"Because it's one of the most beautiful pieces of art every created. And it suits your body tone and shape perfectly."

"So it's a recognizable piece of art? Are you going to paint me as the Mona Lisa?"

"I'm not *that* good an artist," I laughed. "It's pretty hard to match Da Vinci's level of skill. Besides, you didn't sound too thrilled about my painting your face, and that picture is all about the face."

Molly returned placing a small makeup kit on my table and asked if I needed anything else. I shook my head and she circulated around to the next table where the man with the jockstrap was being covered in a liberal coating of black paint.

Batman, I nodded. *Not very original, but I suppose it's every little boy's dream to play their favorite superhero fantasy.*

I flipped open the dish of eye shadow and drew the brush over the powdery paste then stood up directly in front of Bree.

"Close your eyes for a moment," I said.

"Normally I use a soft green," Bree said, lowering her long eyelashes.

"Who's the artist here?" I teased. "You'll have your chance soon enough to mess with me. For now, just stand still and let me do my job."

"I'm looking forward to it," she grinned.

I swiped the brush over each of her eyelids to create a light dusting of lavender color, then reached over to the table for the lipstick cylinder. Bree opened her eyes and smiled at me as I leaned in to apply the gloss.

"I feel like a movie star being primped for the big show. Shall I vamp while you're preparing me?"

I suddenly felt a warm rush between my legs. I was beginning to fall for this girl's personality. Her saucy attitude belied her initial sense of modesty.

"Just shut up while I attempt to make you even prettier than you already are," I said.

As I pressed the tube against her soft lips, Bree opened her mouth, exhaling her cool breath onto my face. My panties suddenly moistened and I flushed slightly.

Bree looked me straight in the eye as her pupils dilated wide as saucers. Apparently, *both* of us were getting turned on by my intimate touch. It took every ounce of my willpower not to close the short distance between us and kiss her on her mouth. The wet gloss hung seductively on her rosebud lips, and I had to bite my tongue to force myself to pull away. When I turned around to retrieve the compact containing the blush, I leaned over at the waist to give her a premium view of my tight ass.

Two can play this game, I thought, turning my face to disguise my widening grin.

When I stood back up with the blush pad in my hand, Bree smiled at me, recognizing how excited I was.

"It looks like one of us doesn't need any help in this department," she said, peering at me through half-closed eyelids.

"You're just getting me all flustered with your sassy attitude. I bet the Mona Lisa didn't give Da Vinci this much trouble while she posed for him."

"He had fewer distractions, as I recall. Wasn't she full clothed?"

"So you have some familiarity with classical art, after all," I said, patting the blush pad gently on each side of her face.

"Just a little. I had to take one course in art history as part of my liberal arts program."

"Where are you studying and what's your major?"

"UC, Public Relations."

My mind suddenly wandered to my last webcam chat with Holly, who was also a student at the University of Chicago. With her red hair and little freckles, Bree even looked at bit like her. I pinched my thighs together imagining her naked with her legs spread apart playing with her wet pussy while I watched her on my computer.

"Is everything okay?" Bree said, noticing my sudden distraction.

"Yes. It's just that you reminded me of someone I know."

"Another one of your muses?"

"In a manner of speaking," I said. "But let's get back to you. I need to concentrate on the matter at hand."

Bree looked at my trembling hand still holding the blush pad and clasped her fingers around my wrist.

"Your hand looks a little shaky right now. Do you need to take a little rest?"

"I'll be fine," I hesitated. "This next part doesn't require the same degree of...personal contact."

I turned back to the mixing table and poured a small amount of red paint into the yellow bowl and blended it with a stir stick. Then I dipped the widest brush I could find in the gold mixture and began swiping the front of Bree's body. As the brush flipped over the edge of her sports bra, it splattered a few drops under her chin. I reached for a towelette on the table and dipped it in the water then wiped her neck with a frown on my face. Bree noticed the other couples painting their fully nude partners, and she grabbed my wrist again.

"You know what?" she said. "This is silly wearing all this getup for a bodypainting class. It's just getting in the way and making a mess. Everybody else doesn't seem to mind getting naked. Why don't I lose the bra and panties? You'll just be covering me up soon enough anyway, right?"

"Um—yes," I said, feeling my heart begin to race at the prospect of seeing her fully naked. "By the time I finish adding all the intricate details of my design, it will be almost impossible to tell that you're actually naked."

"What the hell. Let's do it then."

Bree hooked her thumbs around the side of her one-piece bra and stretched it down and over her body to avoid spilling any gold paint on her face. Then she bent over at the hips and pulled her panties down to the floor, stepping out of them nonchalantly. When she stood back up, I couldn't help ogling at her beautiful figure. Her perfectly bald pussy was framed by slender but shapely hips, and her small breasts were capped with large pink areolas that looked like little cupolas atop her half-domes. To top it all off, her pointy nipples extended almost another full inch from the surface of her skin, echoing the Cathedral of Florence with its pointy lantern atop its peach-colored dome.

Perhaps I should have stuck with a Renaissance-themed design after all, I thought, admiring her classical beauty.

"Still think you can disguise this under all that yellow paint?" Bree said, raising another eyebrow at me.

"I think so. But it's almost a shame to cover you up. You're already a masterpiece just as you are."

"Stop—you're swelling my head," Bree smiled.

"That's not the *only* body part that swelling around here," I joked.

"If you're talking about my funny-shaped breasts, I'm already self-conscious enough about them. I'll be glad when you have them covered up again."

I peered into Bree's eyes, wanting to hold her.

"You shouldn't be the slightest bit self-conscious about your breasts. Believe me, I've seen quite a few in my day, and those are some of the sexiest and prettiest ones I've ever encountered. If I were you, I'd be showing those off every opportunity I could."

"I guess I'm not quite as experienced as you are. I'm still getting comfortable in my own skin."

"Well, let's paint some clothes on you then so you don't feel so uncomfortable."

I dipped the big brush in the gold paint bowl then slowly swiped it over Bree's torso and upper thighs, stopping just below her knees and over the edge of her shoulders. As I watched the hairs of the brush separate over her pointy breasts, I imagined it was my fingers caressing her instead. I was glad that I was wearing a painter's smock to disguise the inevitable wet patch that I was sure was spreading once again in my tight jeans.

"Is that better?" Bree asked.

"Much," I purred. "It's smoother and slicker. Not to mention *sexier*. Which is perfect for the character I'm painting."

"So you're painting a yellow dress on a red-headed model and it's a recognizable portrait of a famous artist. Can you at least tell me in which *century* it was painted?"

"I think I've already told you too much," I said. "If you've taken a course in art history, you could probably narrow it down pretty fast if I told you that."

"What about the *style* of painting? Is it expressionist, cubist, realism, or something else?"

"There's no way I'm giving you any more details. Though if you've seen this painting before, you'll probably figure it out pretty quickly once I start adding the details."

"Do you want me not to look down while you're painting me to maintain the surprise?"

"Yes, please. There must be plenty of other distractions around the room to keep your interest."

"Mmm, yes, I noticed. There are some pretty interesting designs taking shape. You might have some serious competition."

"Well it's not really a contest," I said, dipping my brush into the black paint bowl, "so I'm not too worried about that."

As I sat down on my stool and started to paint the vertical stripes on her stomach, I began to wonder about Bree's sexual orientation.

"But now that you mention it, which ones do you find most interesting?"

Bree took a minute to scan the room, then paused for a long moment peering into the opposite corner.

"Superheroes seem to be a popular theme. There's a Batman, Wonder Woman, Supergirl, and a Catwoman. It looks like we're the only outliers in the room."

I glanced up at Bree's face and noticed her staring intently at one of the models.

"You seem fixated on one in particular. Who are you looking at right now?"

"The two ladies in the far corner. The pretty one is being painted as Catwoman."

"You're not attracted to the naked Batman at the station next to us?"

"He's interesting too. But there's something about that woman's figure. She looks incredibly sexy with her naked body all covered in black."

I dipped a fine hair brush in the red bowl and leaned in to circle Bree's areolas with a flower petal design.

"Do you find yourself attracted to women particularly?" I said, fishing for details.

"I hadn't thought about it very much before today," she said, drawing a slight gasp when I touched her sensitive nipples. "But I have to admit these women look especially sexy dressed up in their naked costumes."

I cleansed my brush in the water bowl, then dipped it in the blue paint and dabbled it softly over Bree's pointed buds.

"Is it turning you on?"

Bree sighed as I circled her nipples with my moist brush, and she began to sway her hips unconsciously.

"Not as much as what you're doing to me right now."

"I'm just getting started," I said. "We've still got a lot of ground to cover. I haven't even gotten to your most inter-esting parts."

"I'm already buzzing in anticipation."

The further I moved down Bree's body with my brush, the more her hips gyrated in excitement. By the time I began painting the floral arrangement on her mound, I noticed thin rivulets of lubrication streaming down the inside of her thighs.

"Have you ever been with another woman?" I probed.

"Only in my dreams. I've never actually been with *anyone* before."

I glanced up from my stool, surprised to hear that she was still a virgin.

"Is that why you came to the body painting workshop?

To explore what it would be like to feel the touch of another woman?"

"Maybe," she said. "I thought it would be a safe place to watch and explore other people's bodies without the pressure of having sex."

"I see your point," I said, facing directly in front of Bree's crotch. "I find it incredibly sexy too." I sensed that she was ready for the last stage of my composition. "Can you spread your legs for me a little bit so I can apply the finishing touches?"

"So soon?" she said. "I'm enjoying this far too much for you to stop now."

"We can always come back for more at the next session. Besides, I have a feeling you might like this next part."

As Bree shifted her legs apart, I pressed my brush between her thighs and drew the soft hairs over her glistening labia. She closed her eyes and moaned softly, tilting her mound upward. I dipped my brush into the bowl of red paint, then flicked it gently over her swollen clit.

"Oh!" Bree panted. "That feels so good. Caress me more with your soft brush, Jade."

Even though I'd covered most of Bree's body and had pretty much finished my design, I lingered for a few moments longer in the sensitive area between her legs. Gently stroking her clitoris with circular motions of my brush, I gradually increased the pressure and speed on her sensitive nub. As I listened to her soft moans and sighs above me, her hips swayed in increasing intensity along with my movements. I was incredibly turned watching her get off from the simple touch of my brush, and I fought the urge to lean in and press my face closer to her.

Suddenly, Bree grasped the top of my head with two hands and began jerking her hips directly in front of my face. I could hear her grunting softly above me, trying not to draw too much attention to our corner of the room. I squeezed my legs tightly together under my painter's smock and enjoyed a long, silent orgasm along with her. I waited until she came down from her climax before withdrawing my brush, then I looked up seeing the flush roll over her face.

"Did you enjoy that, baby?"

"God, yes," she panted. "I want you so bad. I can't wait to touch you at our next session. I've been fantasizing this whole time about how I want to caress you in return."

"We don't necessarily have to wait that long if you want to continue our partnership. I feel exactly the same way about you."

Bree looked down and smiled at me.

"I suppose we should finish up here first. Are you just about done?"

"Just a little bit of final clean up," I said, noticing the yellow paint running down the inside of her thighs. I reached for the moist towelette and rubbed the streaks falling below the hemline of her painted skirt, then reapplied some last-minute touch up where the paint had rubbed off between her legs. As if on cue, Molly moved to the front of the room to address the group.

"It looks like everyone is nearing completion of their compositions," she said. "This is always one of the most exciting parts of the workshop, where each partner gets to reveal their finished work. If you're feeling comfortable sharing, who'd like to go first?"

The Wonder Woman couple raised their hands, then moved their easel out of the way for the rest of the room to see. The model spread her legs and crossed her forearms in the famous pose, as the rest of us cheered. Just as in the poster, the black and gold outline of the "W" emblem across her chest disguised the girl's naked form, but we could still make out the shape of her breasts from the shadows cast by the overhead lights. She was wearing a short blue skirt to cover up her private parts, but she still looked stunning with her painted-on high red boots and epaulets.

"That one looks familiar," Molly said. "Very nice work. I particularly like the golden tiara painted on her forehead. Very convincing. Who's next?"

The Supergirl model stepped forward with a simple blue top and red skirt ensemble and famous red "S" emblazoned across her bare chest. She raised her arm in the Supergirl pose and flapped her cape, giggling her bare breasts under the S emblem.

"We have lots of strong female role models, today," Molly nodded. "I like your use of props to complete the package. Very pretty." Molly turned to the Batman couple and smiled. "I see we have another famous superhero in our midst."

The Batman hunk growled as he assumed the famous pose with his fists clenched by his sides. He'd brought a rubber cowl and cape to match the rest of his uniform and looked every bit the part of the Christian Bale character from the movies. The only distraction in his costume was where his codpiece protruded in his painted-on blue shorts, but we all cheered him on nonetheless.

Next to present was the pretty lesbian woman in the Catwoman costume. Unlike the other models, she was completely nude and painted in black from head to toe. We all ogled her sexy figure, paying particular attention to the sexy cleft between her legs where we could see the slit in her pussy when she spread her legs. Bree wasn't kidding when she said she was the hottest model in the room.

But when it came our turn to present, everyone gasped

when I moved the easel blocking Bree's design. We were the only ones with a portrait concept, and everyone oohed and aahed at the intricate composition. I'd been careful to disguise Bree's private regions with floral designs, but you could still tell she was completely naked if you looked closely enough. She seemed to revel at everyone staring at her, but she still didn't know what she'd been painted as.

"Another exquisite piece of work," Molly nodded, admiring our design. "Now I think it's only fair for each of the models to see their partner's handiwork," she said, wheeling a large wardrobe mirror to the front of the room. "If each of you would like to take turns in front of the mirror, I think you'll be pretty impressed with the finished product."

As each of the models stepped up in front of the mirror, their eyes widened at the realism of their designs. They primped and posed as their partners took pictures of them for posterity. Nobody seemed the least bit self-conscious that a bunch of strangers were watching them stand buck naked as they channeled their superhero alter-egos.

When it was Bree's turn to view herself in front of the mirror, she smiled a huge grin when she recognized the familiar image of Gustav Klimt's famous painting titled The Kiss. She looked absolutely shimmering in the gold and black motif, with red- and blue-colored floral arrangements embellishing her golden tunic. Although she was completely nude, the strategic placement of the black and colored patches made it almost impossible to distinguish her private spots from the rest of her body.

"I had a feeling this was what you were painting," she said, turning her body from side to side. "With the gold and black paint and all the hints you were dropping, I knew it had to be Klimt."

"Are you disappointed I ruined the surprise?" I said.

"Not at all. It's a gorgeous design. You're a very talented painter, Jade. Can you take a photo of me with my phone? I want to remember what this looks like before I have to wash it all off."

I held Bree's phone up and snapped a few pictures, then I handed it to the Catwoman model who'd moved in closer to admire Bree's figure.

"Would you mind taking a picture of the two of us?"

I asked Bree to kneel on a nearby stool, then I moved behind her and dipped my head down over her shoulder and kissed her face just like in the famous original composition.

"What a perfect way to end our class," Molly said, as everyone cheered. "If you'd like to clean yourself up before you leave the studio, we have special lotions in the changing room to help you remove the oil-based paint. Feel free to use the private cubicles if you need any assistance from your partners. I hope to see you all again soon where you can switch roles and paint your other partner with equally pretty bodypaint designs."

As I continued holding Bree in my arms in the kiss pose, I whispered something into her ear.

"Did you need any help removing all this getup?" I asked.

"Yes," she sighed, peering deeply into my eyes. "I want to feel the *rest* of you touching my naked body."

As I pressed my hips against her bare pussy, her tunic design imprinted onto my smock, making us appear as two unified lovers surrounded by the golden fold of her gilded cape.

Soon, my love, I thought, feeling her warm body pressing against mine. *Soon we can dispense with this play acting and be real lovers.*

3

HIDING IN PLAIN SIGHT

After our session ended, Bree and I showered together in the change room where I helped her remove her body paint. While it was disappointing to remove the intricate design, we enjoyed rubbing out bodies together as we channeled the two lovers kissing in Klimt's portrait. I gave Bree two more powerful orgasms running my fingers over her smooth pussy under the warm shower spray.

While we waited impatiently for our next scheduled bodypainting class, we texted back and forth exchanging ideas about what design theme she'd like to use when we switched roles. We searched together online for ideas about how best to highlight my fuller figure while still maintaining a little mystery about my naked form. The trick seemed to be in adding extra detail around the private parts to distract attention from all the extra curves and bulges.

Bree fantasized about painting me as Mystique from the first X-Men movie. She thought Rebecca Romijn's body looked hot and well-camouflaged under the thick layers of dark blue paint. I preferred more playful themes, my favorite showing two hound dog faces painted over one model's huge breasts, with their red noses hiding her erect nipples. But as I scrolled through the nude models on Google Images, all I could think about was Bree's unusually puffy nipples resting atop her perky little breasts. I must have cum a hundred times remembering how it felt sucking on them in the shower of the body-painting studio.

By the time our next session rolled around, I felt closer than ever to Bree and couldn't wait to feel her caress my naked body with her brush. When we arrived back at the studio on our appointed day, I was happy to see a new lesbian couple had joined our group. Bree seemed to have a special affinity for the female form, and I was hopeful the extra distraction would elevate her interest in deepening our relationship.

As with the first session, Molly greeted each couple as they arrived, then she locked the door and closed the window blinds to preserve our privacy. When she addressed the group, she announced a new theme for today's class.

"Welcome back to our returning couples, and to our new couple, Jenna and Lexi."

I noticed Bree sizing up the young lesbian couple, and when one of the girls smiled back at her, I felt a tinge of jealousy.

"Today," Molly continued, "we're going to work with a different type of paint called liquid latex. It goes on thicker and is more durable, so you can wear it longer and even wear it home to show your loved ones. It also can also be fashioned to look like clothing, so it makes the perfect camouflage if you're looking to create an optical illusion. Some of our clients even leave the studio wearing nothing but their body paint to test the realism of their designs."

One of the young lesbian girls raised her hand with a question.

"Yes, Lexi?" Molly said.

"Is that the same kind of paint that was used to design Mystique's costume in the X-Men movie?"

"As a matter of fact, yes. And if you've seen that movie, you might remember how good a job the paint did hiding the fact that she was completely naked in all of her scenes. I must warn you though, that this paint is harder to remove than the oil-based compound we used in our last session. You'll need to use a special body wash to loosen the film, then peel it gently off your skin. Also, if anybody is allergic to latex, you'll want to avoid contact with it. Otherwise, this new paint form can be a lot of fun to work with. As before, choose a painting station to work at, then decide which of you will be the painter and who'll be the model. I'll be floating around offering suggestions and providing assistance as needed. Just let me know whenever you have any questions or need anything. Have fun and let your imaginations run wild!"

Bree and I chose a spot near the window next to the Batman character from our previous session. He smiled at Bree remembering her sexy Kiss design from last time, and she blushed slightly, turning away.

"So, have you thought any more about how you'd like to paint me?" I asked, stealing her attention away from the hunky guy. "Maybe you didn't have such a bad idea about the Mystique character from the X-Men movie after all."

Bree paused for a moment, glancing at some of the design templates hanging from the easels scattered around the room, then flipped through a few posters on our tripod. She stopped at a picture showing a sexy woman wearing a painted-on business suit. Although the design highlighted every curve of her figure, the lapels and seams of the suit provided just enough camouflage to make it seem at first glance that she wasn't naked.

Bree raised an eyebrow and smiled at me.

"The instructor said that some people choose to wear their designs right out of the studio. Something like this might be kind of fun to test people's reactions outside the workroom. Plus, it doesn't look overly complicated for a newbie artist like me."

I glanced at the design on the easel and felt my pussy beginning to throb, imagining myself walking buck naked down the street dressed as a business executive.

"That could work," I said, trying to conceal my excitement.

Bree noticed my erect nipples poking against my thin blouse, then she peered back up at me.

"If you're going to show this to people outside the studio, did you want to wear anything underneath or do you want to be entirely naked?"

"You've already seen me in my birthday suit," I smiled. "I might as well go au naturel in my new business suit."

"I was hoping you'd say that," Bree said, running her eyes over the rest of my body. "I've barely been able to keep my thoughts off your gorgeous figure ever since we shared that sexy shower after our last painting session."

"Oh?" I said, feeling my panties beginning to moisten imagining Bree fantasizing about me while we were apart. "Did you touch yourself while you were thinking of me?"

"Many times. I couldn't wait to get my hands back on you."

"Or at least your *brush*," I said, glancing at the array of painting equipment on the worktable.

Bree looked into my eyes with a lopsided grin.

"From what the instructor said, you're going to need a lot of hands-on help removing the paint when we're done. It could be kind of fun removing your sexy outfit at the end of the day."

I hadn't thought about that aspect of the procedure until Bree mentioned it. The idea of her peeling off my clothes to reveal my naked body underneath sounded like almost as much fun as the business of painting it on. It would also be the perfect pretense to take her home with me and spend some more quality time with her.

"Okay," I said. "You've talked me into it. Why don't you prepare your materials while I get myself ready?"

As I began to disrobe, I watched the other models around the room removing their clothes. The butchy girl from the older lesbian pair had large pendulous breasts, and I wondered what theme her partner would use to highlight her fuller figure. I resisted the temptation to suggest the hound-dog faces, chuckling to myself imagining how it might look on the chunky woman. The Batman couple had also decided to switch roles, and my eyes widened as I watched his sexy girlfriend undress. She had a pretty ballerina's figure and I couldn't help staring as she wiggled her tight ass out of her skinny jeans.

One station further away, the other couple from our previous class had also switched positions, and this time the young man chose to go fully naked for his bodypainting experience. As I watched his large, semi-erect dong swinging between his thighs, I wondered how his partner could possibly disguise his oversize package with any kind of realistic design.

The new lesbian couple were cute and young, and I would have been happy to see either one of them strip naked and display her body for the rest of the group to see.

When the dark-haired beauty stepped out of her loose pantsuit, I was surprised by how large and firm her breasts were. I was glad they'd positioned themselves at the opposite corner of the room where they'd be less of a distraction to Bree. I wanted her attention only focused on me, and I shifted my position a few feet to my left to ensure her line of sight would have minimum diversions.

When she swiveled around on her stool and saw me standing buck naked in front of her, she gasped.

"God, Jade," she panted. "You're even more beautiful than I remember."

"Really?" I said. "It's not like you haven't seen me naked already."

"Well yes, but that was in the close confines of the shower stall while we were standing up washing each other." I watched her eyes dart across my bare mound and flicker between my thighs. "I didn't realize how smooth your skin is. How do you manage to keep yourself so perfectly bare down there?"

"With a little help from my dermatologist," I chuckled. "Laser hair removal is a wonderful thing. If frees you up from having to undergo those frequent painful waxings at the esthetician's office. I'll never have to worry about growing unsightly hairs anywhere in that region ever again."

Bree leaned in to examine me closer.

"And there's no stubble or bumps either. You've given me a perfectly smooth canvas on which to draw my masterpiece."

I looked down at Bree with a mischievous grin.

"If you do a good enough job, I might even let you tear it off me later too."

"I can't wait. But don't distract me. I'm going to need my

full concentration to do a worthy job painting this gorgeous piece of sculpture."

She turned to study the picture of the businesswoman on the easel then peered back at me.

"Do you have a preference for what color of suit you'd like?"

"Well, if I'm going to walk out of here in this getup, the least we can do is match the shoes with the outfit. I always carry a pair of black pumps in the car in case I break a heel, so either black or dark blue might work."

"Let's go with navy blue," Bree said. "I'm going to channel that sexy Rebecca Romijn body one way or the other."

I smiled at Bree's flattering comparison.

"You're going to have your work cut out for you disguising my body as well as her makeup artists did, but I'm up for it if you are."

"Do you prefer a pantsuit or a jacket-and-skirt design?"

"Let's go full pantsuit. It'll look a bit more convincing when I spread my legs. That is—if you think you can properly disguise my kitty."

Bree glanced between my legs and noticed my swelling clit poking out between the top of my labia, then peered up at me and smiled.

"That could be a bit of a challenge, but I'm looking forward to giving that particular part of your body a little extra attention." She motioned to her side table filled with bowls of paint. "You're the expert artist here. What colors do I mix to create navy blue?"

I looked at Bree's collection of bowls arranged with the same colors I'd set up from our last session.

"You can either mix black or orange with lighter blue. But you'd need an intermediate step to create orange by mixing red and yellow, so try black first. Pour a little bit of black paint into the blue paint bowl then mix it up to see how it looks. You can always add more if necessary."

Bree did as I suggested, then lifted the contents of the blue bowl for me to see.

"How's this?"

"Still a little too blue," I said. "I think we need just a touch more black to create true navy."

Bree poured a bit more black paint into the blue bowl and mixed it with the wooden paddle.

"How about now?" she said, tilting the edge of the bowl toward me.

"Perfect," I nodded.

"This first part shouldn't be too hard," she said, glancing at my naked body. The only question is what you want to wear under your suit. Do you want to go bare-chested and reveal maximum cleavage, or shall I also paint a blouse under your jacket?"

"Well, if we're going to take this outside, I suppose the less bare skin showing, the better. It's going to be difficult enough to disguise that I'm nude without drawing extra attention to my bosom."

"Okay," she said, not sure how to blend the two elements. "Should I paint the blouse or the jacket first?"

"I think you'll find it easier to paint the blouse first. You can cover the top half of my chest with white paint, then use the blue paint to draw a V-shape over it to simulate the open lapels of the jacket."

"Will you guide me along the way so I don't screw up too badly? I'm going to need a little help around the neck and with the seams to create an authentic-looking shirt."

"No worries," I said. "Just start by drawing a little band of white paint around the back of my neck, then when you get to the front, create a little V to make it look partially unbuttoned."

"What about the collar? How do I create the little flaps pointing down to the sides?"

"I'll help you when you get there. Don't worry about making it perfect. Most of the fun is in drawing it on the skin, remember? Besides, you can always wash off the paint while it's still wet if you make a mistake. Just go with it. Trust your eye."

Bree tensed her mouth into a little frown, then dipped a medium-width brush into the bowl with the white paint. Then she stood up and moved around my backside as I felt the wet brush slide along the back of my neck. She moved slowly at first, trying to create a perfectly straight line around the diameter of my neck, then exhaled heavily when she turned around to face me again.

"Whew," she said. "It's harder than I imagined drawing a straight line on a curvy surface. Now for the tough part."

She paused for a moment, looking at my neckline and large breasts, trying to imagine how a real blouse would look on my chest.

"How much cleavage do you want me to show?"

"Just enough to maintain interest but not enough to draw undue attention to that part of my anatomy."

"Okay," she said, holding the brush with a trembling hand next to my collarbone.

"Just taper the line gently into a closed V," I said. "Remember that an open blouse has a bit of a naturally wavy line anyway, so it doesn't have to be perfect."

Bree inhaled a deep breath, then slowly drew the brush down the front of my chest over the top of my breasts. I tried to remain still while she painted me, but I could feel myself shaking as the most hairs of the brush slid over my bust.

"Now for the other side," she said, repeating the process on the left side of my chest.

When she finished, she stood back and appraised her work, nodding softly.

"I think that looks about right. Now I just need to fill in the side panels and the collar."

As Bree continued to work on me, Molly circulated around the room and joined our group. She glanced at the design Bree had chosen on our easel, then looked at her work-in-progress on my upper body and smiled.

"Looks good so far," she nodded. "Did you need any help, Bree?"

"Actually, yes," Bree said. "You arrived at the perfect time. I'm trying to paint a faux blouse on Jade's chest, but I'm not sure how to create the proper edges to form the points of her collar. Can you help me?"

"Absolutely," Molly said. "The key is to adjust the shades ever-so-slightly to create the illusion of shadows at the edges of each element. Why don't I do the right side for you while you watch, then I'll guide you as you do the other side?"

"That would be perfect, thank you," Bree said.

"If you look closely, you can see that the first coat of white paint has a slight pink tinge to it from Jade's bare skin beneath. All you have to do is paint over the area in question with one or more coats to brighten the whiteness. Let me show you."

Molly chose a finer-point brush from the table then dipped it into the bowl of white paint. Then she leaned in close to me and drew a short V-shaped design pointing down to my left breast. She seemed laser-focused on drawing the design, and I was disappointed not to see her gaze stray at any time down toward my naked breasts. She repeated the sequence a couple of times, painting over the same area to brighten the white color. Then she mixed a bit of black paint with the white on the mixing palette and drew a small outline around the edge of the collar.

"Using just a little bit of light gray color around the bottom edge of the collar simulates a natural shadow effect and makes the fold stand out a little more prominently."

She stood back and surveyed her work then looked at Bree.

"What do you think? Does it look like a realistic collar?"

"Absolutely," Bree said, with wide eyes. "That's incredible how easy you made it look. Can you stay and watch me while I try the other side?"

"That's what I'm here for," Molly said. "I think you'll find it's easier than it looks."

Bree picked up the fine white brush and began slowly drawing it over my right collarbone. I could see that she was holding her breath the whole time as she got redder and redder in the face, then she looked up at me as she drew away. I blew her a gentle kiss and mouthed the words 'you're doing great'. She stood back comparing the two sides and squinted her eyes.

"I can see it beginning to take shape," she frowned. "But it still doesn't look as natural as your side."

"You just need to add a bit of gray shadow around the corners, like I did," Molly said. "You might go a few more centimeters further around the edges though, to mimic the deeper shadow coming from the other side of her body."

As Bree touched up the other side of my collar with the gray brush, I watched Molly's eyes as the darted up and down my chest from my exposed breasts back to Bree's brush. I smiled when I caught her eye and wondered if we'd have a chance to see her naked before we finished our body-painting program. I remembered Liz mentioning in our original online chat that we might have a chance to work with edible paint at some point, and I hoped that there might be an odd number of participants at our next session so I'd have a chance to see her naked body close-up.

After Bree finished applying the gray shadow around the edge of the collar, she stepped back and furled her brows in disappointment.

"It still doesn't look as natural as your side," she said, shaking her head. "What have I done wrong?"

Molly took the brush from Bree's hand and stepped back in toward me.

"You just need to feather the grayness slightly as you move further from the tips of the collar, like this."

I felt Molly draw the brush gently down the front of my chest closer toward the top of my breast, then she glanced up and smiled knowingly at me as she assessed the design.

"What do you think?" she said to Bree. "Does that look a little more convincing?"

"It's perfect," Bree said. "Can you come back a little later when I get to the jacket lapels and seams? I might need your assistance to create the proper shading with the blue paint also."

"No worries," Molly said. "Just remember to paint over the areas you want darker and use a slightly modified shade to create the necessary shadows. I'll come back in a few minutes to see how you're doing."

After Molly left, Bree looked at me with wide eyes and exhaled through puffy cheeks to emphasize how difficult the painting process was.

"You're doing fine, girl," I said. "If the painting expert says it looks good, I'm sure it will pass the man-in-the-street test. Just keep doing what you're doing and it will come out fine. I'm just enjoying watching your pretty face contort into all these sexy expressions while you're touching me with your little brush."

"Isn't it supposed to work the other way around?" she said. "I want to make your face contort into sexy expressions while I'm touching *your* naked body."

"All in due time," I said. "I'm enjoying the buildup. Believe me, I'm getting incredibly turned on watching you do your handiwork."

"Maybe I can make you feel a little more so as I move lower down your body," she said, winking at me seductively.

Bree moved on to highlight the two sides of the seam running down the separated halves of my blouse, then dabbled a bit of gray into the white paint to draw the buttons on the placket. Then she grabbed the widest brush and dipped it into the navy blue bowl and began swiping it over my breasts.

"Now we're getting to the fun part," she said, peering into my eyes as they glazed over in pleasure.

"Yes," I purred. "Paint me, Bree. Slap that wet brush all over my tits. God, how I wish I could fuck you right now."

"All in due time," she said, mimicking my taunts from our last session. "We still haven't gotten to the interesting parts."

"Mmm, I can't wait," I said, continuing our little game of cat and mouse.

Bree continued swiping the thick brush down the front and back of my body, pausing briefly around my wrists and ankles to draw a straight hemline at the bottom of the sleeves and pant legs. Then she selected a finer brush to draw the V-shape at the front of the jacket outside the edges of the white blouse she'd painted earlier. I could feel the white paint starting to harden as it stuck to my breasts, feeling like a stretchy rubber film on my skin. I looked down and saw that my nipples were swelling, stretching the film into two shiny, frosted teats.

If this is what it feels like for a guy to wear a condom, I thought, *this isn't such a bad feeling*. I was getting more and more turned on as Bree covered my body with this sexy second skin.

When she finished painting the basic outline of the pantsuit, she paused for a moment, studying the picture of the model on the easel. She glanced again at the shading around my blouse collar, then chose another fine-point brush and dipped it in the black paint bowl. Then she leaned in closer to me and traced a diagonal line from my left shoulder over my left nipple, toward the center of my chest.

"Whatever you're doing now, I like it," I sighed, feeling the wet brush tickling my erect nipples as it flicked over my raised points.

"I'm highlighting your jacket lapels, so be still so I can get the lines right. I'm trying to use the black shadow to disguise your big nipples, so no one will know you're actually naked."

"They're not as big as yours," I said, glancing at Bree's chest covered by her splatted apron. "You have the most sensuous, swollen areolas I've ever seen. I can't wait to feel them back in my mouth when we're done with all this."

"It sounds like you've had a lot of girls' nipples in your mouth," she said, glancing up at me briefly.

"Well, not really that many," I backpedaled nervously, as a blush fell over my face.

"Don't worry," Bree said, glancing over my shoulder at the nude model at the next station over. "Your secret will stay with me. I'm kind of glad you've got more experience with girls. It just makes you a better lover, where you can teach me all the tricks."

"You have *no* idea," I said, smiling at her devilishly. "I've only just begun to share some of my girl-loving secrets."

"I'll look forward to that," Bree said, noticing the blue streaks running down the inside of my thighs. "But right now, you better put your dick back in your pants. I need you to stay composed while I finish your wardrobe. At least until the paint dries."

"Yes ma'am," I said, staring at the front of her smock, trying to distract my attention from her pretty face.

For the next twenty minutes, Bree sat facing me on her stool as she used the black paintbrush to outline the front and bottom seams of my suit jacket. I could feel the brush sliding over my skin from the center of my navel toward the edges of my hips. She seemed to be finding her confidence now, moving more quickly as she leaned back periodically to appraise the unfolding design. But when she began drawing a straight line down the front of my mound to high-light the shape of the fly on the front of my pants, I couldn't stop moving my hips as my clit buzzed in anticipation. When she stopped just shy of my throbbing nub, I peered down at her, disappointed.

"I thought you were going to spend a bit more time down there," I said. "My love button is dying for some special attention. Doesn't it need a special disguise too?"

Bree paused, holding her black brush inches from my glistening pearl, trying to decide how to best camouflage the parted folds of my swelling labia.

"Spread your legs," she said. "I think I know just the trick."

I shifted my legs apart and Bree drew a straight line from

the crack of my ass to the bottom of the fly seam just above my clit.

"That's it?" I protested. "That's all the attention you're going to give me down there?"

"I don't want you to get too excited. You'll mess up my perfect design. But I'm not quite done yet. Spread your legs a little wider so I can see what I'm doing."

I widened my stance another foot apart and inhaled slowly, thinking Bree was going to tease my love button with her brush from the extra room I was providing. But instead, she tilted her head and drew a fine line down the inside of both thighs all the way to the bottom hemline of both legs. Then she grabbed the gray brush and swiped it gently over the side of my shinbones. When she finished, she stood up and appraised my body from top to bottom. Molly rounded the corner and nodded approvingly at Bree's composition.

"Very nice, Bree," she said, admiring the design. "I see you've taken my guidance well on how to create the appropriate shading to highlight the edges of the lapels and seams. That was very clever the way you drew the jacket lapels over Jade's breasts to disguise her nipples. Did you have any other questions before we wrap up?"

"Just one thing," Bree said, focusing on the front of my chest with pinched eyebrows. "The lapels still look a little flat, like they're, well, *painted* on. I've tried outlining them already with a black color. Have you got any other ideas as to how I can make them look a bit more natural and realistic?"

"I think so," Molly said. "Once again, it's all about using different shades of the base color to create subtle shadows mimicking the natural fall of light on the different angles of the fabric. The lapels naturally curve over a woman's chest, reflecting more light from above. You just need to use a lighter shade of navy to create the illusion of the natural fabric. I'll demonstrate once again on Jade's right side, and you do the left."

Molly dabbled some navy paint into the mixing palette then dabbled a swish of white paint into the mixture to lighten it slightly. Then she took a medium-hair brush and swiped it a few times down the right side of my chest and stepped back.

"See how that highlights the lapel slightly, making it seem to bend and curve naturally in the light?"

"Yes," Bree said. "Thanks for your help. I think I can take it from here."

Molly looked up at the wall clock showing we only had only fifteen minutes left in our session.

"How much more time do you need?"

"Just a couple more minutes, then we'll be done."

Molly handed Bree her brush and she dipped it back into the mixture, then she carefully swiped the brush over the other side of my jacket lapel. She stepped back and nodded at the final result, then reached over for the fine-point brush on the table.

"It just needs one more finishing touch," she said.

She dabbed the brush into the bowl of white paint, then she leaned back in toward my chest and drew a thin horizontal line directly over my right nipple.

"Well it's a little too late for that," I sighed in mock disappointment. "But I'll take whatever I can get at this point."

"I think you'll be happy with the final result," Bree said, smiling into my eyes. "We can always have more fun playing with you later. Right now, I'm excited to show you the finished product. I think you look absolutely stunning in your custom-tailored business suit."

When everybody had finished painting their designs,

Molly drew our attention to the front of the room and had each model pose once again for the group.

The chunky lesbian girl had been dressed as a clown, which actually looked superrealistic with her oversized circus shoes, spongy nose, and curly red hair. The batman couple had flipped roles, with the girl painted this time as Batgirl, which didn't seem terribly inspired, but nonetheless looked sexy on her slim and shapely frame. The guy with the big dick was dressed as a fireman, with a thick coil of hose painted over his shoulder. A loose section of the hose dangled down the front of his torso, with the open end strategically positioned directly over his thick organ. I nodded at the creative placement of the brass fitting on the end of the tube used to disguise the exposed glans of his penis. Someone would have to look twice to notice from a distance that he was stark naked. I smiled, thinking how much fun the couple might have with this design after they went home and charged up his firehose with a little extra pressure. The young lesbian couple chose to go with another cartoon superhero theme, this time using the Joker's quirky sidekick Harley Quinn as their muse. Bree and I both lingered for a few extra seconds ogling her girlish figure, recalling the sexy image of Margot Robbie from the recent movie, *Suicide Squad*.

When it came our turn to present, everyone commented on how realistic the suit looked on my body, and when I looked in the full-length mirror, I was floored at how good a job Bree had done. The shadows around the shirt collar and jacket lapels made the design seem to stand out in 3-D relief, and the positioning of the lapel edges and pant seams made it almost impossible for someone standing at a distance to notice my prominent breasts and bare pussy. She'd even added a white pocket square over my breast patch to help disguise my protruding nipples. I'd never been more excited in my life to show my naked body to someone, and I was eager to test how well it would pass the public scrutiny of strangers outside the studio.

"You did an incredible job!" I said, turning to give Bree a big wet kiss.

"Do you really think so? Do you think it's fairly realistic?"

"*Fairly?* I bet I could sit at the end of a boardroom table and hardly anyone would tell I was naked. Let's give it a try and see what people in the street think!"

"You mean walk out of here just like *that*?" Bree said with wide eyes.

"Absolutely. What's the worst that could happen? Get arrested for public indecency?"

"That, and a major traffic pileup from rubberneckers gawking at your gorgeous body."

"Only if they figure out that I'm actually naked. Come on, let's get out of here and have some fun!"

4

EN PLEIN AIR

Bree and I pranced out of the art studio giggling like two schoolgirls. I stopped to fetch my black pumps from my car, then we walked arm-in-arm down the sidewalk of the local street. A few oncoming cars passed by without any sign of recognition, then one of the drivers on my side of the street stepped on his brakes and craned his neck into his rearview mirror as he passed by. We stopped at an intersection waiting for the light to change, and someone on the opposite side honked his horn when the lead car paused unusually long at the green light. When we stepped onto the crosswalk, an older woman approaching from the other side smiled at us, then her eyes opened wide when she realized that I was naked.

"This is crazy," Bree said, looking at the stunned look on the faces of passing motorists.

"It's not so bad," I shrugged, turning my head to assess the oncoming traffic. "So far I've only noticed a couple of people recognizing me. This road is too quiet to do a fair test. Let's turn down this busier street and see how many heads turn. It's much more liberating than I imagined walking outside without any clothes."

"It'll only seem liberating until a cop pulls over and throws you inside his paddy wagon."

"You only live once," I said, hooking my other arm through Bree's and pulling her across the adjacent cross-walk. "Let's live a little dangerously!"

As we began to walk along the side of the busy boulevard, most of the motorists passed by without incident, but after a short time, more and more drivers slowed down and honked their horns when they realized what was going on. By the time we approached the next intersection, men were cat-calling at us through their open windows and weaving dangerously across the road. When we got to the light, I heard the sudden screech of tires and the sound of crunching metal behind me. Bree and I looked over our shoulders, and when we realized it was only a minor fender-bender, we scampered across the intersection to the other side.

"I *told* you we were going to cause a traffic jam," she said. "Haven't we had enough fun already? Let's get out of here before someone gets seriously hurt."

I glanced around me, noticing the accumulation of pedestrians staring at us from the other side of the inter-section.

"Okay, but where can we go? It's at least a twenty-minute walk back to our car."

Bree heard the sound of a passing overhead train and looked up.

"Let's take the El to the next stop. It'll bring us closer to the studio, and at least get us off the street."

"And be packed in a sardine can with a bunch of leering

passengers?" I said, beginning to feel increasingly self-conscious from so many prying eyes upon me.

"It shouldn't be too busy at this time of the day," Bree said. "We'll can find a spot in the corner and I'll stand next to you to provide cover."

She glanced over her shoulder at the two bickering motorists, pulling me toward the transit station entrance.

"Let's get out of here before the police arrive."

The station wasn't as busy as I feared, and we passed through the turnstiles without incident as other commuters hurried up the escalator to catch an incoming train. Bree stood below me on the moving stairs to block the view of other people riding behind, and I crossed my arms over my chest as passengers riding the opposite escalator gawked at my unusually tight-fitting clothes. I was glad we were able to step inside the arriving train as soon as we reached the platform. We found an empty corner of the carriage and sat on a side bench facing away from the rest of the compartment.

"Whew!" Bree giggled, squeezing my hand tightly beside me. "That was a close one. I was afraid that guy from the accident was going to blame you for the crash."

"We're still not entirely in the clear," I said, glancing nervously around the compartment. "What if a transit cop sees us? I'm pretty sure riding in the nude on a public train is against the rules."

"Just be cool," Bree said, noticing the other passengers scattered around the car staring at their phones. "Nobody's noticed you yet, and we're all alone on this side of the car."

She looked down at my crossed arms and legs and smiled.

"You know, I've barely had a chance to look at you from a distance since we left the studio. Do you mind if I sit on the opposite side of the aisle and take a few pictures? It'll be kind of cool to have some photos of a nude businesswoman riding the train to work."

"What the hell," I shrugged. "Might as well milk this thing for all it's worth while the going is good. Just don't leave me alone if more passengers come down this way."

"Don't worry," Bree said, smiling at me reassuringly. "I'll protect you from any peeping Toms."

She stood up and walked over to the adjacent bench seat and reached into her purse. Then she held up her camera and tapped the screen.

"Don't look so stuffy," she said. "Uncross your arms so I can see your pretty tits. There's no point going out in public like this if you're not going to flaunt it a little bit."

I uncrossed my arms and placed my hands in my lap, not knowing where to put them. In my haste to get away from the studio, I'd stowed my purse and other belongings in my car. It felt strange to be sitting in a public venue without my phone or any other personal effects, making me feel even more exposed.

"That's good," Bree smiled, as she tapped her screen to take a few pictures. "Now spread your legs a little bit. Imagine you're riding to work and you're trying to steal the attention of a pretty girl on the other side of the train."

"Like *this* one," I said, nodding toward Bree as I parted my legs.

"Exactly. Imagine she can see between your legs and notices you're not wearing any panties. See if you can get her to squirm in her seat while she looks at your sexy naked body."

I parted my knees further and placed my right hand on my crotch as I began to rub my nub under the dry latex paint. The coating felt strange to my touch, like when I was washing dishes wearing rubber gloves. But this sensation was a whole lot more enjoyable than cleaning dishes. As I felt my button begin to swell under the tight film, the buildup of juices around my pussy made a seductive squishing sound.

"*Yes*," Bree said. "Just like that. You are so turning me on. Can I take you home with me when we're done here? I've been fantasizing about fucking you ever since our first painting session. I want you to teach me all your girly moves."

I smiled at Bree, pointing my toes to spread my legs wider.

"If I wasn't covered in this tight film of paint, I'd show you one right now," I said, wanting to plunge my hand into my sopping pussy and finger-fuck myself while she watched me. But I was thankful to have the coating of paint protecting my bare skin from all the germs on the public transit seat.

Just then, the train roared into the next station and the doors opened as more passengers streamed into our end of the car. I shook my head at Bree, wondering if she wanted to exit at this stop. She noticed a folded newspaper in the corner of her seat and quickly threw it across the aisle to me. Two passengers took positions on opposite sides of each of us, and I unfolded the paper and crossed my legs, holding the tabloid over my chest.

With the paper concealing most of my upper body, neither of the new passengers seemed to notice that I was sitting bare-naked directly in front of them. Bree looked at me and smiled with a devilish grin. I was beginning to enjoy this process of play-acting like a regular commuter, and Bree tilted her head sideways, encouraging me to uncross my legs again. I furrowed my eyebrows, watching the pretty girl next to her clicking her thumbs on her smartphone.

Bree frowned and mouthed the words *'You only live once'* to me.

I lifted my knee and slowly parted my legs, shuffling the paper to distract attention from my shifting position. But the noise caught the attention of the girl next to Bree, and she looked up from her phone and did a double-take when she noticed the deep cleft between my legs created by my swollen labia. I froze in terror, realizing that she'd found me out, then she looked up and smiled at me before tapping on her screen with increased urgency. It was obvious that she was texting someone about what she'd just seen and I glanced at Bree, rolling my eyeballs to my side to indicate that her seatmate had discovered me. Bree looked down out the corner of her eyes at what the girl was tapping on the screen and smiled at me.

'She thinks you're hot!' she mouthed.

Suddenly Bree's brows furrowed and the color went out of her face as she realized the girl was opening the camera app on her phone. She held her fists out in front of her chest and raised them a few inches, signaling for me to cover my face. When the girl tilted her phone toward me, I crossed my legs and spread the paper as wide as I could to conceal my identity. As much fun as I was having playing this little game of striptease, the last thing I needed was for an image of me sitting naked on the subway going viral all over the internet.

When the train rushed into the next station and the doors opened, I stood up and rushed toward the exit. I'd had enough of sharing my body with a bunch of strangers, I just wanted Bree all to myself. She followed me out of the car and we paused on the platform to discuss our next step.

I noticed a taxi dropping someone off at the station entrance below the platform.

"Let's grab a cab and go home," I said. "I think I've had quite enough of this exhibitionist routine. It's time to get out of these clothes and feel your naked body next to mine."

"I was thinking the exact same thing," Bree said. "Do you want to go to your place or mine?"

"I need to go somewhere safe and comfortable. Do you mind coming to my place? We can always go back to the studio to pick up our cars a little later."

"I'm in no rush," she smiled. "Except to feel your bare skin again."

***

As soon as we got to my place and I closed the door behind us, I turned around and pinned Bree against the frame. As I pressed my body against her and kissed her passionately, I rubbed my burning clit against her hip.

"Fuck, that was hot," I panted. "That has got to be one of the sexiest things I've ever done."

"No kidding," she said. "Did you see the look on that girl's face when she realized you were naked?"

"I almost had a heart attack when I realized she was trying to take a picture of me. What was she typing on her phone?"

"Something about this hot babe sitting naked in front of her on the train. She told her friend you were gorgeous and that you were turning you on."

"Did that get you turned on too?"

"Are you kidding me? I almost came when you started touching yourself."

"Let's go upstairs," I said. "Help me get this stuff off so I can properly make love to you. I'm damp as a dishrag under all this plastic coating."

"Can we leave it on just a little longer?" Bree asked. "I want to fantasize about the business executive having her way with me before you go back to your normal identity."

She lifted her finger to my mouth and pulled my bottom lip down.

"You still have a few open bare patches where we can have some fun."

"As long as you help me peel this off all the *other* spots where we can have even more fun."

I took her by the hand and led her upstairs to my bedroom, then laid her atop my comforter.

"Now it's *your* turn to spread your legs," I said. "I've been dreaming of sucking your pussy ever since I covered you in yellow paint at our first workshop. Let me show you what it feels like to be properly made love to by a woman."

"Yes, boss," Bree grinned. "Teach me the right way to do the job."

I pushed Bree's torso down on the bed, then began to unbutton her blouse. It was lightly splattered with blue paint around the collar, and I smiled remembering how pretty she looked as she concentrated on painting me.

"The first thing to remember," I said, getting back into character for our play-acting scenario, "is to not rush an important task like this. The key is to tease your subject, so her arousal level slowly builds up until she's begging for you to touch her."

Bree looked at me with a playful expression.

"What if she's *already* seriously turned on from all the foreplay we've just been through?"

I paused, peering at her with a lopsided grin, then I grabbed the two sides of her blouse and ripped it apart, revealing her bare breasts.

"Then you dispense with any unnecessary effort and seize the opportunity when it reveals itself."

"Hey!" Bree protested in mock indignation. "That was one of my most expensive blouses. Now you're going to have to give me a raise."

"Oh, I'll give you a *raise*, alright," I sneered, leaning down to suck her puffy areolas into my mouth.

As I sucked on her teats, I could feel them swelling in my mouth, and after a few moments I lifted my head and stared at her unique double-domed breasts.

"That's my girl," I panted. "God, how I love your pointy breasts. Do you like it when I suck on your pretty tits?"

"Yes," Bree sighed. "Show me how to properly lick a woman's breasts. I want to learn everything from you so I can return the favor when it's your turn."

"Mmm, yes," I smiled. "Soon enough. But since this is your first time, I think it's only fair that I spend a little more time with you. Lie back while I worship your beautiful temple."

I placed my mouth back over Bree's swollen nipples and circled my tongue around her tips as I felt them harden and press further into my mouth.

"That feels so good, Jade," Bree moaned. "Don't stop. Suck my big pink nipples. Hold me like the lovers in Klimt's painting."

"I couldn't touch you the way I wanted while I was painting you," I said, moving up to kiss her lips. The brush can only accomplish so much. You've got to lose yourself in your painting in order to truly appreciate it's beauty."

"Yes, Jade," Bree panted. "Lose yourself in me. I want to feel you become one with me just like the lovers in the painting."

Seeing the flush in her pale cheeks, I bent down and

began kissing her down the front of her torso. As I passed her breasts, I reached out one last time and squeezed them gently, rolling her thick nipples between my fingers. I could have spent all day playing with her tits, but her gyrating hips told me she wanted my attention elsewhere.

When I reached her navel, I unfastened the button at the top of her jeans then I unzipped her pants and pulled them off her legs. She was wearing gold-covered lace panties, and I smiled remembering what it was like to touch her there while I painted her at the studio.

"You shouldn't have," I purred, looking at her bare skin under the lacy threads.

"This time you can *remove* the yellow from my body rather than covering me with it."

"That's exactly what I was thinking," I said.

As I curled my fingers under the top of her panties, she lifted her hips off the mattress and I pulled them softly down her thighs. This was the first time I'd seen her pussy fully exposed from below, and I gasped when I saw how delicate it looked. She had the prettiest puffy folds of symmetrical lips running along both sides of her slit and not a single hair follicle in sight. With her pale, perfectly bald skin, her cunny almost looked like a little girl's, and I felt the latex covering sticking to my snatch as my pussy began to water like an open faucet. I could see the head of her clit poking out from its sheath, throbbing in the glistening overhead light.

"God damn, Bree," I panted. "Just when I thought you couldn't possibly get any sexier. That's the prettiest pussy I've ever laid eyes on."

"I'm glad you like it. I spent a lot of time today getting myself properly prepared. I know how you like it smooth and bald."

"I do," I said. "It's as smooth as a baby's bottom."

"Lick my bare pussy, Jade. Show me how to make love to a woman."

"Oh, Bree," I said. "You have no idea how much I've wanted to do this. Just lie back and enjoy."

I lowered myself onto the bed between Bree's legs and began kissing her thighs up toward her mound. The closer I got to her pussy, the wetter her skin became as her lubrication streamed down her legs. I moaned, remembering the image of the yellow paint running down the inside of her thighs when I brushed her bare vulva in the workshop. I lapped up her sweet nectar and closed my eyes savoring the fresh scent.

When I reached her pussy, I flattened my tongue and licked the front of her slit like an ice cream cone up and down a few times, as Bree made soft mewing sounds. Then I closed my lips around her soft labia and sucked her flesh into my mouth. Bree spread her legs wider for me, and I nibbled my way up toward the apex of her folds. When I finally reached her burning clit and closed my mouth around her, she gasped and pressed her mound into my face.

"Oh God," she moaned. "It feels incredible to feel your lips around me. I'm going to come, Jade. Hold me close."

I was surprised that Bree was ready to climax so quickly, but I knew that this was her first time experiencing cunnilingus, and I was thrilled she was so turned on by my touch. Her hips jerked softly against my face as she grunted above me, and I pressed my tongue against her bud, feeling it tremble in my mouth. I held her gently while she came down from her high, then I pulled myself up beside her and peered into her blushing face.

"That was fast," I said.

"I've never felt anything like that before," she said. "That's way better than doing it by hand."

"Even with a wet brush?" I said, smiling into her eyes.

"Well you were giving me a little more focused attention down there this time. Speaking of which, I promised you more of that at the studio. Can I return the favor now?"

"By all means," I said. "But I think you'll have to help me off with my clothes first. I'm probably covered in who-knows-how-many germs from the subway seat."

Bree peered back at me and smiled.

"Maybe I only need to remove a little flap over your strategic areas. Let me enjoy this little fantasy for a little longer."

I kissed Bree softly, feeling the wetness building up in my crotch.

"Okay, but I have a feeling you won't need any special moisturizer to loosen things up down there. I'm already soaking wet between my legs."

As Bree wiggled her body down beside me, she kissed and licked the sticky paint covering my torso. When she reached my breasts, she squeezed them gently and flicked her tongue around my nipples just I'd done with earlier.

"What does it feel like underneath all this paint?" she asked.

"Kind of strange, actually. I can feel you touching me, but everything is kind of desensitized."

"That's not what your *nipples* are telling me," Bree said, noticing my teats pushing up against the stretchy film.

"Maybe this is what it feels like for a guy wearing a condom," I mused. "He can get hard, but it doesn't feel the same as going au naturel. I've always enjoyed the touch of bare skin far more."

"We can arrange that," Bree smiled, noticing my hips beginning to gyrate in excitement.

She lifted herself up and positioned herself between my thighs, then paused for a moment to study her handiwork.

"It almost seems a shame to take this off," she said. "I drew the paint seam so perfectly right over your crot—"

"If you don't tear these off me soon," I interrupted, "I'm gonna jump you and fuck you, pretty pants or not. I'm dying to feel your sweet mouth on my bare lips."

Bree looked up at me with a devilish grin.

"I'm just playing with you. You told me earlier that the key to making love to a woman is to tease her until she's begging for you to touch her."

"You're a quick study, girl," I smiled back at her. "But I think you've gotten me properly warmed up. Now get down there and show me some love."

"Yes boss."

She spread my legs further apart, then she dug her fingernails into the sides of my vulva and drew them down toward my bottom. I could feel the rubbery film stretching, then I felt a rush of cool air as the seal broke over my wet pussy. It was an exhilarating feeling being exposed in this raw condition to Bree, but I worried that the lack of fresh air to my covered pussy over the last couple of hours might create an unpleasant smell.

"It feels so good to let my pussy breathe again," I said. "But it must stink down there after being all closed up this long."

Bree moved in closer and began to peel the layer of film away from my perineum.

"Not at all," she said, inhaling a deep breath through her nose. "You just smell...*sexy*."

"At least it should be *clean* down there," I said. "Nothing else has touched me since I showered this morning."

"Let's see if we can remedy that situation."

When I felt Bree's lips touch my pussy, I moaned as I tilted my hips up to meet her lips.

"God, I needed this so bad," I hissed. "I feel like I've been freed from a cage. Suck my pussy, baby. Make your boss cum with your pretty lips."

She proceeded to nibble and tease my labia as I'd shown her earlier, then she placed her lips over my raging clit and sucked me into her mouth.

"Yes, Bree," I panted. "Suck my clit. It feels so good."

Bree circled my pearl with her tongue, then she began flicking it up and down in a repeating pattern. I lifted my head and pulled her head up gently.

"Don't forget to mix it up a bit, baby," I said. "A girl likes to feel like she's being worshipped down there, not trilled by a teenage boy. Pretend you're licking a lollypop. Sometimes you suck on it, sometimes you lick it, and sometimes you roll it around in your mouth. It's the *variety* that turns your partner on."

"Sorry, Jade," she said, looking up at me with her wet face. "This is all so new for me. I'm glad you're teaching me. I want to learn how to satisfy you. Keep telling me what you like while I lick you."

She placed her face back between my legs and rolled my nub around her mouth, alternating between licking and sucking. As I began to feel my passion rising, I rolled my hips on the bed and moaned in excitement.

"That's perfect, Bree," I panted. "I'm getting close. Make love to me with your mouth."

I reached down with my two hands and pulled her face tighter against my pussy. It didn't take long for me to reach the point of no return, and I lifted my hips off the bed as I cupped Bree's face in my hands.

"I'm going to come for you baby," I groaned. "I'm gonna cum so hard in your mouth."

When the wave finally poured over me, I whinnied like an injured animal from the pleasure rolling over me.

"Uhhn," I moaned. "I'm cumming, Bree! Taste me, baby."

As the explosion of built-up lubrication inside my pussy poured out of me, I felt my juices spraying against the side of my thighs and all over Bree's face as I held her tightly against me. My contractions lasted for almost a full minute while I jerked and heaved my hips in the throes of climax. When I finally collapsed my body back onto the bed, Bree lay transfixed watching my vulva continue spasming until I exhaled heavily, signaling the end of my powerful orgasm.

"That was so hot!" she exclaimed, shimmying up excitedly beside me. Her looked like she'd devoured a messy watermelon. "I didn't know a girl could squirt like that. You almost *drowned* me with your juices."

"Sorry, baby. I can get pretty wet when I'm turned on. I think I had quite a bit pent up inside me from all the foreplay leading up to this. When you made me cum so hard, it just gushed all out of me."

"So I did a pretty good job for my first time, boss?" she said, smiling at me.

"Yes, baby," I said, peering into her pretty green eyes.

I placed my mouth over her glistening lips and tasted my sweetness coating her face.

"And next time," I said, remembering that we'd be using edible paint at our next painting session, "I'll be the one eating you all up."

5

FORBIDDEN FRUIT

I made love to Bree all afternoon, bringing her to multiple new highs worshipping her tender body. I wanted her to spend the night, but she was beginning to experience cramps from all the powerful orgasms she'd experienced, and she had mid-term exams the next day. In the intervening days leading up to our next bodypainting class, we texted back and forth like lovestruck teenagers, teasing each other about what we planned to do at the next session.

I went online and scrolled through hundreds of images of nude bodypainting models, but by the morning of our class, I still wasn't sure what theme I'd like to use. It was Bree's turn to be the model again, and I was looking forward to playing out our fantasies in front the whole class. I wasn't sure how far Molly would allow us to explore our partners in full view of the other participants, but I had a feeling the addition of edible paint would create some strong temptations.

When Bree and I arrived at the studio, three of the couples from the last session were already there and they asked us about our experience testing our business suit design in the street. The young lesbian couple seemed particularly interested in where we went, and when we told them about our train experience, their eyes widened in excitement. Everybody seemed more charged up than usual for today's class, but I noticed the fireman stud from the previous session kept tapping his phone while he glanced out the front window impatiently. As we neared the appointed start time, Molly asked where his girlfriend was and he said they'd had a fight and wasn't sure she'd attend. When she offered to step in to be his painting partner for today's session, he took one look at her sexy body and nodded sheepishly.

At ten a.m., she looked outside the front door then latched it shut and slowly pulled the blackout blinds over the windows. I was glad she was being more careful than usual, because I knew if any passersby had any inkling as to what was going on inside, they'd be pressing their noses to the glass. When she was certain we had complete privacy, she went to the front of the room to address our group.

"As I mentioned at our last class, today we're going to change things up with a different type of paint. This time, we're going to use a special type of edible paint that will allow you to have a little more fun when I comes time to clean up. But I should warn you that this paint isn't quite as durable as the oil and latex paint we used previously, so it can get a bit messy and runny if you leave it on for too long.

"Also, in the interest of sharing the spoils with everybody, I encourage you to switch roles halfway through the session so that *both* partners will have a chance to be participate in the fun. As always, all your necessary materials are laid out for you at your respective painting stations, and you've got additional design ideas to browse through on your easels."

Molly looked over at the fireman stud and smiled.

"It looks like Brett will be on his own today, so I'll be pairing up with him for today's session. But if any of you need any help at any time, just give me a shout and I'll pull away for a few moments. Before we get started, do you have any questions?"

One of the young lesbian girls put up her hand.

"Yes, Lindsey?"

"What exactly is the edible paint made from? I mean, how safe is it to—*eat*?"

Molly nodded her head with the familiar question.

"You might be surprised to find that it's made from the same ingredients as store-bought Jello pudding. It's a blend of milk, sugar, cornstarch, butter, and vegetable-based food dyes, totally non-toxic and safe to eat. Although it might be a little cool to the touch at first, since it's been kept refrigerated to keep it from spoiling. But that just makes it all the more titillating to apply. Were there any other questions?"

The girl from the Batcouple pair raised her hand timidly.

"Yes, Kate?"

"Are we allowed to, you know, *sample* our creations from time to time as we work on them?"

Molly's lips curled into a sly smile.

"That's the whole point of using edible paint. Half the fun is in removing it once you've finished your design. We realize that some of you may find it difficult to contain your excitement as you're being painted. If you want to explore your creation more closely at any time, we've tried to provide a safe and open environment to do so."

Molly paused as she looked around the room.

"But if anybody is going to feel uncomfortable about seeing others touch their partner's body in this way, now is the time to say so. We don't want anyone feeling self-conscious about either watching or being watched as we explore this fun facet of the bodypainting experience. Of course, if you want some additional privacy, you're also welcome to use our private change rooms in the rear."

Molly paused to make eye contact with each workshop participant to be sure everyone was comfortable with the rules of engagement.

"Does anybody have any more questions before we get started?"

Everybody looked at their partners and nodded with crooked grins on their faces. Bree and I moved to the nearest painting station and flipped over a few design panels on the easel to generate ideas. The themes seemed to be divided between the main food groups. Most of the male models were painted in fruit or vegetable themes, with the strategic placement of various tubers and legumes used to disguise their hanging genitalia. Many of the female models were painted in dessert themes, with cherry-topped sundaes and other sundry pastries used to disguise their private parts. But we both paused when we saw a picture of the sexy Latin actress Carmen Miranda wearing a skimpy costume of grapes and berries with a fruit bowl perched atop her head.

"What do you think?" I said, looking at Bree. "Are you hungry for the main course, dessert, or a little appetizer?"

"As much as I like the idea of licking all those yummy-looking pastries off you, I think the vegetable and fruit themes might be a little easier to paint."

I glanced at the picture of Carmen Miranda and nodded.

"You might be right, but remember what Molly said. This session isn't so much about trying to create a perfect design as it is about having fun and enjoying the cleanup process. It's just going to get all smeared off soon enough, anyway."

"Mmm," Bree smiled, thinking back on how we rubbed our bodies together when she was at my place. "I like the idea of smearing it off each other. Who should go first?"

I turned to the front of the room and saw Brett beginning to strip in front of Molly.

"Why don't you go first so I can guide you along the way? I have a feeling Molly's going to have her hands full for most of this class. Besides, I've got a little surprise embellishment that I have planned for the end."

"Oh?" Bree said, widening her eyes in curiosity. "I thought you'd already showed me all your tricks when I was at your place."

I smiled at her with a raised eyebrow.

"A good lover likes to mix it up from time to time, remember? Plus, I like to save the best for last. Kind of like the cherry atop the ice cream sundae."

"So you were thinking of painting me in a dessert theme? I've been dying for you to lick my cherry again."

"You'll have to wait and see," I said. "Just try not to melt until I finish. This particular surprise will require a stiff upper lip, so to speak. Go get yourself ready while I strip."

"Yes, boss."

As Bree popped the lids off the glass jars of pudding paint, I glanced around the room to see how the other partners were progressing. The Batgirl at the next station over had chosen a meat theme to paint on her hunky boyfriend as she began to paint sinewy slabs of steak over his bulging pecs. The young lesbian couple was going with the pastry theme, as I watched one of the girls lean in closely to paint pretty pink cupcakes over her girlfriend's breasts.

The middle-aged couple had chosen a playful seafood-based theme, as the slender one began to paint an image of a school of fish swimming across her partner's undulating chest. Molly was painting another meat locker theme on Brett's gym-toned fireman's body. I glanced down at his thick Johnson swaying between his legs and noticed it twitching as she began moving her brush down his body.

"So, what'll it be?" Bree said, swinging around with her brush in her hand. "Citrus fruit up top and strawberries down below?"

"Sounds about right," I smiled. "Melons to cover my big parts and berries to cover the little ones."

"What do you think about grapefruits to cover your breasts? They're pink and sweet, and about the right size."

I paused, remembering some of the images I'd seen while surfing online to get ideas before the workshop.

"That could work," I said. "But did you know there's a special type of fruit grown in Southeast Asia that looks almost exactly like a woman's bare breasts? It's called milk melon, and it's incredibly erotic. Here, let me show you."

I reached into my purse on the floor and pulled out my phone, then tapped on my screen a few times.

"See?" I said, turning the screen around for Bree to view the images.

The picture showed a bamboo trellis with long flesh-colored bulbs hanging down from the vine. At the bottom of the spoon-shaped plants was a swelling with a darkened circle in the center that looked amazingly like a bare breast.

"It might be kind of fun to paint a bunch of these on my chest to make me look like I have multiple boobs. It would be hard to distinguish the real ones from the fake ones."

Bree took a look at the screen and jerked her head back in amazement.

"That's a *real* fruit?!" she asked. "They look exactly like a woman's breasts!"

"Yes, except for their elongated shape. But that just makes them look all the more erotic, like some kind of Salvador Dali painting."

"No kidding," Bree said. "Talk about a surreal image. I'm not sure if this is going to make you look more sexy or *creepy*!"

"It won't seem so creepy when you're sucking on those fake breasts once they're painted on my chest. Get to it girl. The clock is ticking."

"Okay," Bree said. "Just help me figure out how to blend the paint to create that unique color."

"Place equal parts of red, yellow, and blue on the mixing plate, then mix them together. You'll want to make it slightly darker than my skin tone so they stand out more clearly on my chest. If you need to lighten it, just add a bit of white to the mix."

Bree mixed the paint as I suggested, then dipped a medium-width brush in the blend and held it up to my chest.

"Here's goes nothing," she said. "Are you sure you're ready to have three breasts?"

"The more the merrier," I chuckled.

"All the more to suck on," Bree smiled.

She leaned in began slowly drawing the brush down from the base of my neck toward the center of my chest. When she reached the top of my cleavage, I could feel her moving the brush in circles as she stared intently at the design. Then she swiped the brush up and down the center of my chest a few times and stepped back and glanced at my phone to compare it to the photo.

"That was easier than I thought," she said. "It about the

right color, and it stands out in nice contrast to the rest of your skin. Now I just need to add the fake nipple. Red and white makes pink, right?"

"You got it, girl."

Bree mixed the new shade, then used a finer-point brush to paint the darker nipple in the center of my new breast. She circled over it a few times to create the proper shading and shadow, then stepped back and nodded.

"Not bad, if I do say so myself," she said. "It almost looks like your real breasts."

"Just a lot more pendulous," I chuckled.

"Good point," Bree said. "We'll need to touch up your real ones a little bit to create the surreal effect from the image."

Bree leaned back over the mixing table and dabbled the brush in the flesh-colored paint, then turned around and began painting some lines above each of my breasts. Each time her brush reached the top of my tits, she paused and feathered the paint to blend in with the lighter shade reflecting from the lights overhead.

"I kind of wish we'd gone with the grapefruit theme," I frowned. "You're barely even touching my actual breasts this time."

"That's part of the *look*, remember? We're trying to mimic fake boobs alongside your real ones. They'll get plenty of attention later when I suck *all* of your breasts when we're done."

Bree proceeded to paint a few more faux breasts on the top and side of my chest, then she stepped back and compared her design with the photo one last time.

"I think I've got the gist of it," she nodded. "It looks pretty much just like the melons in the photo. Shall I paint the bamboo shoots behind them to simulate the look of a trellis?"

I looked up at the clock and noticed that forty-five minutes had already passed.

"I think you better move on to the lower part so we don't run out of time. I'm dying to feel your brush again on my clit. Besides, we still have to allow a bit of time at the end for the fun part."

"Oh yeah," she said. "For the *surprise*."

Bree glanced at the picture of Carmen Miranda on the easel, then began mixing a darker shade of pink to simulate the color of cherries. As she began painting the belt of hanging fruit around my waist, I glanced around the room again to see how the other teams were doing.

The Batcouple had almost finished painting the hunky guy in their deli-case theme, with mouth-watering cuts of ham, turkey, and beef covering his shredded abdomen. His girlfriend had cleverly angled a turkey roast over his crotch so that one drumstick extended down his thigh while the other one rested over his throbbing organ. I glanced over to the other side of the room, where the young lesbian girl sat on the edge of the mixing table with her legs spread apart as her partner kneeled in front of her painting a white cake with strawberries over her mound and pussy.

"Hurry up, Bree," I said. "I'm starting to get hungry. I can't wait to eat you all up."

Bree smiled at me as she dipped the fine-point brush in the pink paint mixture, then she sat down directly in front of me and began painting strawberries around my vulva. When her wet brush touched my clit and she began swirling it around in little circles to paint another berry, I sighed in pleasure.

"Keep doing that and you're going to make me come," I said.

"I better stop then," she said, smiling up at me. "I

wouldn't want to ruin the buildup. I'm supposed to make you *beg* for it, aren't I?"

"I've taught you too well," I cursed.

Bree stood up and stepped back to appraise her creation, then she took a quick glance at the picture on the easel.

"Not quite as intricate as Carmen's dress, but I think it'll do in a pinch. You definitely look edible."

"Okay, *your* turn," I said, shifting her to the other side of the easel. "Now it's my chance to have a little fun with you."

"Were you thinking of painting me in a similar style?" Bree asked.

"With a slight variation," I said, winking at her. "I think I'll continue with the fruit theme, just with some different types of exotic fruit."

Bree looked at me curiously.

"Does this have something to do with the surprise you mentioned earlier?"

"Maybe," I smiled. "But just like with your Kiss painting, you're just going to have to wait until the end to see what it looks like."

"Damn, Jade, you're such a tease."

"Just like I taught you. Don't you find it makes for a more intense climax?"

"Yes, but maybe you can be a bit easier on me this time. It took three days for those abdominal cramps to go away after I last saw you."

"A lot of women would give their right arm to experience orgasms that powerful."

"I suppose you're right. I guess not *all* girl cramps are bad."

As I began painting my design on the front of Bree's body, she looked around the room, and I noticed a little stream of fluid running down the inside of her right thigh.

She seemed particularly intent on watching the pretty lesbian couple in the far corner, and I wondered just how far along they'd gotten in appreciating their design. After another thirty minutes, I finished painting my composition and stepped back to admire the final product.

Molly had placed full-length mirrors on the opposite side of each workstation easel, and I motioned for Bree to step toward the back of the Batcouple's tripod to assess her completed design. When she looked in the mirror, she smiled at the level of detail I'd put into my concept. The horn of cornucopia tilted down the front of her chest, spilling it's bounty of fruit onto her bare mound and pussy.

"Mmm," she said. "I like how the bowl of fruit points to my kitty. But what's that purple-colored fruit right at the base of the bowl?"

"That's an eggplant."

"Isn't that a vegetable? It looks a bit like a—"

"Penis?" I chuckled, recognizing the familiar shape. "It's definitely a fruit. A very *tasty* fruit when cooked in the right way. But yes, it also makes a very sexy dildo when you're in a pinch."

I reached down into my purse and pulled out a real, eight-inch eggplant. Bree's mouth opened wide when she realized what I had in mind.

"You're kidding?" she said. "You put that thing *inside* you?"

"This one's big enough to fit inside *both* of us," I grinned.

Bree opened her eyes as big as saucers.

"You've been holding back on me," she smiled.

"Hey, a girl doesn't want to reveal *all* of her tricks on the first date."

Bree shook her head as she pinched her eyebrows at me.

"You weren't thinking—*right here*?" she said.

I looked around the room and saw that each of the other

couples were locked in a passionate embrace as they kissed and licked each other's bodies. The lesbian couples were already grinding their hips together and we could hear the moaning of the Batcouple behind their easel. Even Molly and Brett were getting into it at the front of the room, as her head bobbed over his drumstick that was pointing straight up in the air.

"Looks like everybody's gotten a head start on us," I said, placing my hand on her chest. "Lie down on the table so I can properly fuck you."

Bree paused, as she pushed back against me gently.

"Don't you want to see your creation first? Take a look in the mirror at the design on painted on you."

I stepped in front of the glass and gasped when I saw Bree's work. The fake milk melons blended in perfectly with my own artificially elongated tits, giving the impression of multiple swelling breasts covering my chest. I glanced down and nodded at the way she'd woven the strings of cherries around my waist to look like a hanging skirt, then strategically placed strawberries around my thighs to disguise my pussy.

"Very impressive, young lady," I said. "I particularly like the little touch where you added a dab of chocolate-colored paint at the tip of the strawberry right over my clit. Very clever—and very sexy."

"Can I lick it off you before you do me?"

"By all means," I said. "I've been dreaming about you eating my pussy this whole week."

Bree stepped toward me and reached out to cup my breasts, then leaned down and took my left nipple into her mouth. I tilted my head down and looked at the bizarre sight of many fake tits on my chest and moaned.

"Yes, Bree," I painted. "Suck my tits. *All* of my tits."

She lifted her head and began licking the tips of my faux milk melons and purred.

"Mmm," she said, smacking her lips. "They taste wonderful. So sweet."

She licked each of my fake melons clean, then placed her head over my right breast and circled her tongue around my areolas as she rolled my erect nipple around in her mouth like a lollypop.

"You're such a good student," I sighed, recalling how I'd taught her to mix up her technique.

"I studied hard," she said, popping her mouth off my rigid nipple.

"I bet you did," I said, placing my hands around her hips and swinging her over to the edge of the painting table. "Now let me have a little fun with *your* sweet fruit."

I moved the paint materials to the side of the table, then lifted her up onto the edge and kneeled down in front of her. Spreading her legs wide, I drew my tongue up the side of her thighs then licked her dripping slit from the edge of her rosebud all the way up to her steaming clit.

"Fuck, Jade," Bree grunted. "That feels so good. I want to feel you inside me."

I looked up at her and smiled, then slipped two fingers inside her tunnel as I puckered my lips over her nub and sucked her into my mouth. As I began to thrust my fingers inside her, she grabbed the back of my head and began to rock her hips into my face. I could taste the sweet smell of sugar filling my mouth as the dark purple paint began to stream down my face.

"Yes, Jade," she said. "Fuck me with your fingers. I'm so close—"

I pulled my fingers out of Bree's cunny and glanced up at her with my stained face.

"Not yet, baby. I want to feel you pressing up against me when you come. Lean back a bit more."

Bree tilted her back down toward the table and rested her weight on her two elbows as she watched me position the big eggplant in front of her pussy. I slowly inserted the slender end in her opening, then I moved in closer to her and lifted my right leg onto the table beside her. I pressed the thick end of the tuber into my hole and pressed my hips forward as the fruit disappeared inside both of our holes. When our vulvas merged and we felt our clits touch, Bree threw her head back and squealed.

"Oh my God, Jade," she yelped. "That feels incredible. Fuck me with your big purple dildo."

I grunted in pleasure, as much from the incredible sensation of the squash sliding inside me as from Bree's dirty talk. I angled my hips up and began thrusting harder against her hips as we ground our clits against one another. Bree's eyes suddenly glazed over as I realized she was on the verge of coming from the tip of the eggplant rubbing against her G-spot.

"Fuck, Jade," she suddenly screamed. "I'm going to cum! Fuck me with your big cock. Oh God—I'm cummming!"

As I watched a deep flush roll over Bree's pale chest while she bucked wildly against my hips, I listened to the sound of moans and sighs filling the rest of the room. This was one workshop I'd never forget, I thought, as I pressed my mound against Bree's, squirting red and purple paint all over her belly.

Everyone's an exhibitionist in disguise...

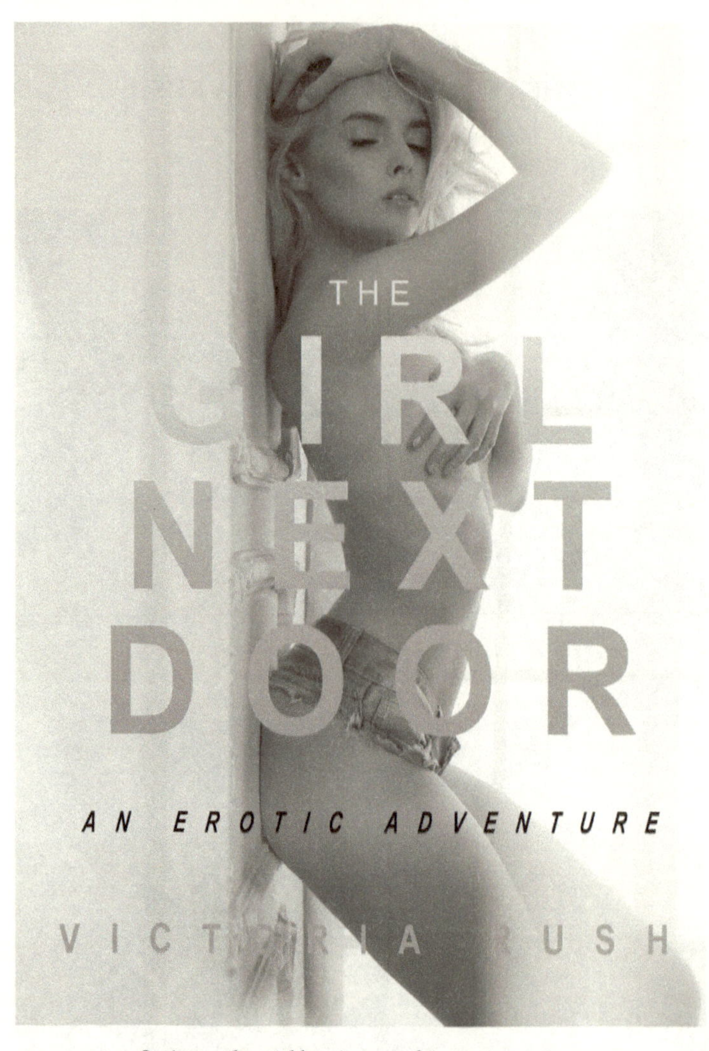

Spying on the neighbors just got a lot more interesting...

Some habits are harder to break than others...

Everything's sexier in the dark...

GIRLS' CAMP

AN EROTIC ADVENTURE

VICTORIA RUSH

Getting wet was never this much fun...

ABOUT THE AUTHOR

If you would like to receive notification of new books in Jade's Erotic Adventures, follow me at http://bookbub.com/authors/victoria-rush.

If you have a moment, please post a brief review on my Amazon book page at viewbook.at/paintme . Even just a couple of sentences will help other readers find and enjoy this book as much as you hopefully did.

Follow, share, like, and comment at:

www.facebook.com/authorvictoriarush
www.pinterest.com/authorvictoriarush
www.twitter.com/authorvictoriarush
authorvictoriarush@outlook.com

Hope to see you again soon!

THE DINNER PARTY - PREVIEW
FINGER FOOD

Sometime later, I heard a soft tap on my bedroom door. Not wanting to remove myself just yet from my cocoon of luxury, I called out to answer.

"Yes?"

"It's time for your massage," a woman's voice replied.

"Just one minute please."

I reluctantly stepped out of the bath and quickly toweled myself dry. I wrapped a large bath sheet around me, re-donned my mask, then opened the bedroom door.

A petite young Asian girl greeted me, wearing a kimono similar to mine and a crimson masquerade mask.

Apparently not everybody who works here always walks around stark naked.

The girl was utterly breathtaking. Long jet-black hair cascaded over high cheekbones past pouty lips, her delicate collarbones peeking from the top of her kimono. I could see her breasts and hips outlined by the tightly-wrapped kimono and suddenly wished that she too had come to my boudoir naked.

"My name is Jasmine," she said. "I'm your personal

masseuse and esthetician. Are you ready for your final preparation?

Just the thought of this beauty laying her tender hands on me sent a shiver down my spine.

"Definitely. Please come in. How would you like me to prepare?"

"Come with me, please."

Jasmine led me into the bathroom, where she nonchalantly removed her kimono and hung it behind the bathroom door.

Oh my God.

I didn't think anyone in this place could get more beautiful or sensuous. Jasmine had perfectly shaped B-cup breasts with a thin indentation running down the center of her perfectly toned stomach. Like everyone else in this place, her pubis was utterly bald and flawless. She barely looked eighteen and I was just about to ask her age, but she spoke first.

"If you'd like to remove your towel and lay face down on the table, we can get started. May I call you Jade?"

There was something about her confident manner and tone that belied her youthful appearance. I had no inhibitions whatsoever about displaying myself unclothed to this stranger.

"Yes, thank you, Jasmine." I unhooked my bath sheet and threw it against the side of the tub.

"Would you like me to drape your backside?" Jasmine asked.

"That won't be necessary," I quickly answered.

Jasmine walked over to the vanity counter and picked up two small bottles of oil resting under an orange radiant lamp. She brought them back to the massage table, opened one, and poured the oil into one cupped hand then rubbed her hands together. The scent of lavender wafted toward my nose.

I closed my eyes in anticipation of her touch. I'd had massages before, but nothing as sensuous and stimulating as this. When her hands touched the small of my back, I jerked reflexively from the sexual tension. My heart was beating a hundred miles an hour as I felt the blood coursing through my veins.

Jasmine must have sensed my nervous tension and began pressing her fingers more firmly into my back as she moved them slowly up each side of my spine. The warm oil allowed her hands to glide effortlessly across my skin. She used every surface of her hands to massage my muscles, expertly kneading my skin with her fingers and palm.

I began to relax as my muscles softened and surrendered to her touch. She sensuously massaged every part of my back, shoulders, and neck, applying just the right amount of pressure. Periodically, she would pour more warm oil on my lower back, dipping her hands in it to replenish the silky lubrication against my pliant skin.

Just as the sexual tension began to subside from the utter relaxation of the massage, Jasmine moved her hands down to my buttocks and began to caress them in soft circular motions. My glutes contracted involuntarily and I unconsciously pressed my mound into the firm padding of the table. Suddenly I was quickly reminded that a gorgeous young woman was caressing my naked body. She cupped each buttock between her hands as she massaged my ass tantalizingly, her little finger sliding slowly into the cleft just above my anus.

Periodically, I'd partially open one of my eyes with my head turned in her direction to look at her gorgeous body. My head was at the same level as her midsection, and my mouth watered as I watched her stomach muscles flex and her hips undulate with each movement of her hands. At times her pussy was almost right beside me and I wanted to reach out and run my own fingers up her soft legs.

I was in total heaven and getting wetter by the moment. Just when I thought I couldn't stand it anymore, she suddenly moved her hands down to my feet and began massaging her thumbs into my soles.

I'd always loved having my feet massaged, but nobody did it like Jasmine. She cradled my foot and used every part of her hands to massage and knead every surface from my heel to my toes. I didn't want her to stop, but there were other parts of my body that were screaming for attention.

As if reading my thoughts, she began moving her hands up toward my calf, using her thumbs to spread the muscle apart. She lingered almost as long on my calf as she had on my foot, rolling the ball of my calf between both of her hands, sliding her slick hands up and down erotically. I couldn't help imagining how she might use those same hands to massage a man's erect cock in a similar manner. My mind wandered again to what pleasures lay in wait for me over dinner.

After shifting her hands to my right leg and giving my other foot and calf similar attention, she placed each hand just behind my knees and began to slowly move them up towards my buttocks. Her thumbs pressed against my inner thighs as she glided tantalizingly close to my apex.

I rolled my legs outward in an invitation to move closer. My legs were parted enough that I was sure she could see my vulva from her vantage point behind me. In my highly aroused state, my lips were engorged and spread apart, revealing my moist and quivering opening.

But as much as I desperately wanted her to, Jasmine

never touched me there. She repeatedly slid her hands right up to the edge of my slit, pressing and rotating her thumbs on the fleshy meat of my upper thighs just below my aching pussy. I suppose this was part of her master plan—to tease me mercilessly and inflame my passions so I'd be ready for just about anything at the main event.

It was certainly working. After thirty minutes of Jasmine's ministrations, I was grinding my pussy into the table trying desperately to give my clit some needed direct stimulation.

Just when I thought I couldn't be teased any more tantalizingly, Jasmine opened one of the bottles of warm oil and poured it directly into the crack of my ass. She paused as the fluid flowed down and directly over my parted lips. I almost came from the gentle movement of the warm liquid as it trickled across the folds of my labia, channeled toward the junction where they joined together at my clit. I shuddered in pleasure at the feeling, even if it was only the subtlest of touch.

Jasmine suddenly interrupted my thoughts.

"Would you like to turn over now?"

It was the first time she had spoken directly to me since the massage started, and it surprised me in my catatonic, pre-orgasmic state. I practically flipped over like a fish out of water and spread my legs expectantly. Finally, I'd get some relief. Surely, she couldn't leave me hanging like this.

"It's time for your final grooming," she said. "I'll need you to part your legs a bit further to provide full access."

Grooming? I knew this was part of the process, but somehow it didn't seem fair to transition at this precise moment. At least I'd be able to stay on the comfortable massage table instead of the clinical vinyl chairs used by my regular esthetician.

Jasmine walked over to another cabinet by the makeup table and withdrew a leather bag from one of the drawers, then brought it back to the table. She reached into the bag and pulled out a cordless hair trimmer.

"Do you have a preference regarding your appearance?" she asked. "Do you prefer natural, neatly trimmed, or bare?"

I knew she was referring to my pubic hair, which I generally kept neatly trimmed. I'd always thought going fully bald was unnatural and unseemly, catering to men's prurient fantasies of fucking young schoolgirls. But in this situation, it seemed entirely appropriate, like I was stripping away all my camouflage and armor.

If tonight was all about being watched, I might as well bare myself in every sense of the word and truly let my inhibitions go. I began to fantasize about rubbing my bare pussy against Jasmine's while she poured warm oil between us. The more work she had to do on me, the more chance I'd have to make this last and hopefully get off.

I didn't hesitate. "Bare, thank you."

"As you wish," she said. "I'll remove the long hairs first with the trimmer, then shave you smooth with a razor."

No waxing? This was different. I was relieved to not have to bear the painful and violent trial of having my hairs ripped out en masse. Although shaving down there was always a scary proposition, I felt safe in the capable and practiced hands of this beautiful esthetician.

Jasmine nodded, then flipped a switch on the trimmer. The device buzzed softly as she placed it gently on my mound. I had only a light dusting of fur and it didn't take long for her to remove it with a few short strokes over my pubis. I shuddered as the vibrations penetrated deep into my core. If she had placed the flat head on my clitoris, I would have popped off in a millisecond. Instead, she turned the trimmer face-down and gently swiped the vibrating teeth against the sides of my vulva, sensuously separating my labia with her hands as she moved the device between my legs to trim the hairs on the inside and outside of my labia.

It was an insanely titillating feeling, but just clinical enough to bring me down from my plateau and shift my focus. My mind wandered to the upcoming feast, and I contemplated what surprises lay in wait at the main event. The hostesses had suggested there would be 'contact' of some sort during the meal, and I was intrigued exactly who and how it would be administered. The idea of being fully bald, cleansed, and thoroughly stimulated going into the event was an incredible rush.

Jasmine continued with the trimmer all the way down my perineum to my anus, barely touching me with the trimmer so as not to pinch any delicate tissues. Apparently there were no parts of my erogenous zone that would remain untouched, now—and perhaps later.

She turned off the trimmer and placed it at the foot of the table. Then she took a bottle of gel from the bag and spread the gel on her hands. Using both hands, she spread it gently between my legs, starting on my mound all the way down to my rosebud.

My body almost levitated above the table as Jasmine finally laid her hands directly on my clitoris. The gel had a mild stinging quality that added to the stimulating sensation. If this was meant to excite my follicles in preparation for the shave, it wasn't the only feature of my anatomy that it made erect. I could feel the hood of my clitoris retract as my button filled with blood and began to push outward. Suddenly, I was fully stimulated again and lusting for Jasmine's touch. I fantasized about her bending down and taking my swollen nub between her puffy lips and letting me come in her mouth.

Unfortunately, my satisfaction would have to wait a little longer. Instead, Jasmine reached into her bag and pulled out a straight-edge razor. In anyone else's hands, it might look threatening, especially in my prostrated and vulnerable position. But something about the way she delicately and sensuously opened the jackknifed tool instantly evaporated my fears. I could see how this type of razor would in fact give her better control safely cutting my stubs instead of the usual ladies plastic razor.

With her right hand, Jasmine gently laid the razor on its flat edge at the top of my mound, while she gently pulled my skin upwards with her other hand. Then she slowly turned the sharp edge perpendicular to my skin and began softly scraping the razor downwards. I could hear the bristling sound as the razor edge removed my nubs right down to the follicles. She repeated the pattern in one inch wide swipes on one side then the other of my pubis, being ever-so-careful to stop just where my clitoris lay quivering in a mixture of fear and excitement. There was something about the utter vulnerability of the procedure that made it the most erotic experience I'd ever had.

Jasmine used the same deft touch as she moved down my vulva and perineum, scraping the vestiges of stray hairs away with gentle swipes of the long blade, while sensuously separating my folds and flesh with her other hand. She took extra time and care around my anus and clit, using the gentlest and slowest motion I've ever felt someone apply to my body. The combination of fright and titillation as she probed my most sensitive body parts created a river of sensuous fluids running down my vulva. By this time, no shaving gel was necessary to provide a smooth gliding surface for the knife.

When she was finished, Jasmine retrieved a fresh wash towel from beside the sink and held it under the warm water faucet then twisted the excess water into the basin. She returned to the table and placed it over my splayed legs then gently cleansed the excess moisture and remaining shaving gel with gentle massaging movements of her hands. The warm, moist towel felt exquisite against my newly shaved skin. Jasmine's hands now felt comforting between my legs rather than erotic.

She had taken me on an incredibly sensuous erotic arc, right to the edge of ecstasy and back, to a quiet relaxed place. I exhaled fully and completely for the first time in almost an hour.

Jasmine removed the towel from between my legs and held up a large hand mirror at a forty-five degree angle toward me.

"What do you think?" she asked.

I tilted my head up and studied her masterpiece. Far from the usual red and swollen vulva that I typically experienced after the violent waxing with my regular esthetician, I'd never seen my pussy look so beautiful. Utterly bereft of any hair, my entire perineum from my pubic mound to my anus was totally bald, pink—and gorgeous. I just stared at my beautiful pussy, utterly transfixed by the transformation.

"You have to *feel* it to really appreciate how beautiful you are, Jade," Jasmine purred.

I moved my right hand down, running my fingers along the edges of my pussy. I gasped from a feeling I'd never felt before. It felt smooth as silk: no bumps or blemishes or cuts or bruises. It was almost as if I was feeling somebody else—somebody I'd never felt before. I couldn't stop my left hand joining the other in rubbing and caressing my sensitive organs.

Jasmine lowered the mirror and smiled at me as I felt the moisture begin to accumulate between my legs again.

"It's almost time for your dinner appointment," she said. "Why don't you save the best for last? I think you'll find plenty of ways to satisfy your appetite over the next couple of hours."

She lifted my kimono from the hook at the edge of the bathtub and held it open for me.

"I'll escort you downstairs now if you're ready. All you need to bring is your kimono and slippers—and your mask of course."

I sat up slowly and stepped off the massage table. Turning around, I held my arms out as Jasmine lifted one arm of the silk robe onto me then the other. Then she turned around to face me, wrapped the silk tie around me, and tied a single bow over my belly button. She retrieved my matching silk slippers and knelt down on one knee to gently lift my feet one at a time and place them softly inside. It took every ounce of my power not to grab her head and pull it into my pulsating pussy.

Jasmine stood up gracefully and smiled into my eyes.

"If you'll follow me, I'll escort you now to the fantasy feast."

She didn't bother putting her own robe on. Her tight little ass barely jiggled as she stepped smartly ahead of me. I wasn't sure if I'd have a chance to feel Jasmine's touch again before the evening was over, but for now I was in total bliss ogling her petite, curvaceous figure from behind...

Read More